T0083527

Karolinum Press

MODERN CZECH CLASSICS

Ladislav Fuks
The Cremator

Translated from the Czech by Eva M. Kandler
Afterword by Rajendra Chitnis

KAROLINUM PRESS 2016

KAROLINUM PRESS
Karolinum Press is a publishing department
of Charles University
Ovocný trh 5/560, 116 36 Prague 1
Czech Republic
www.karolinum.cz

Cover illustration by Jiří Grus
Designed by Zdeněk Ziegler
Set and printed in the Czech Republic by Karolinum Press
Second English edition, first by Karolinum

Cataloging-in-Publication Data is available from the National Library
of the Czech Republic

ISBN 978-80-246-3290-2 (pb)
ISBN 978-80-246-3334-3 (ebk)

The Devil's neatest trick
is to persuade us
that he does not exist.
Giovanni Papini

I

'*My gentle one*,' Mr. Karel Kopfrkingl said to his beautiful, blackhaired wife on the threshold of the Predators' House as a faint early spring breeze stirred his hair, 'so here we are again. Here, on this dear, blessed spot where we met seventeen years ago. I wonder whether you still remember *where* it was, Lakmé?' And when Lakmé nodded, he smiled tenderly into the depths of the building and said: 'Yes, in front of that leopard over there. Come, let's go and have a look.' After they had crossed the threshold and were walking towards the leopard through the heavy, sweltering stench of the animals, Mr. Kopfrkingl said:

'Well, it seems to me, Lakmé, that nothing has changed in these seventeen years. Look, even that snake in the corner over there is where it was then.' He pointed to the snake in the corner gazing down from the branch at *a very young pink-faced girl in a black dress* outside the cage, 'I wondered then, seventeen years ago, why they put the snake in the Predators' House since there's a special house for snakes ... and look, even that railing is still here . . .' he pointed to the railing in front of the leopard which they were approaching. Then they reached the leopard and came to a halt.

'Everything is as it was seventeen years ago,' said Mr. Kopfrkingl, 'except perhaps for the leopard. The one we saw has probably been called to meet his Maker. Gracious Nature probably freed him from his animal fetters long ago. Well, you see, my dear,' he said, watching the leopard behind the bars who had its eyes half closed, 'we always talk of gracious Nature, merciful fate, benign God. We weigh and judge others, censure them for this and that – that they are suspicious, slanderous, envious and I don't know what, but what we are ourselves, whether we ourselves are kind, merciful, good ... I always have a feeling that I'm doing awfully little for you. That article in today's papers about the father who ran away from his wife and children in order not to have to support them, that's terrible. What's that poor woman and her children going to do now? Perhaps there's some law which will protect her. Laws at least should protect people.'

'There is bound to be such a law, Roman,' Lakmé said quietly. 'I am sure they're not going to let the woman and her children starve to death. You keep saying that we live in a decent humanitarian state where justice and goodness reign. Yes, you say so yourself. And I suppose we're not badly off, Roman . . .,' she smiled. 'You have a decent salary, we have a large, beautiful flat, I look after the household and the children . . .'

'No, we're not badly off,' said Mr. Kopfrkingl, 'thanks to you. Because you had a dowry. Because your late mother supported us. Because your aunt from Slatiňany is supporting us, who, had she been a Catholic, would certainly be canonized when she dies. But what have I done? I've perhaps furnished that flat of ours, but that's all I have done, even if it is a beautiful flat. No, my dear,' Mr. Kopfrkingl shook his head and looked away at the leopard, 'our little Zina is sixteen, Milivoj fourteen, they're precisely at the age when they need most, and I have to take care of you all. That's my sacred duty. I've had an idea how to increase my income.' And when Lakmé looked at him in silence, he turned to face her and said:

'I'll get an agent and give him a third of my commission. Mr. Strauss will do it. It will help you as well as him, my heavenly one. He's a good, tidy fellow. He's had a shocking life. I'll tell you about it later. Who wouldn't help a good man? We'll invite him to The Silver Casket restaurant.'

Lakmé pressed herself against him, her eyes smiling and gazing at the leopard behind the bars whose eyes were still half closed like a big good-natured dog. Mr. Kopfrkingl, too, was looking at the leopard with smiling eyes. Then he said:

'Do you see, my gentle one, animals can feel tenderness. They can be nice when we are able to reach out to them and enter their sad, reserved souls. How many people would become good, nice, if there were someone to comprehend them, to understand them, to caress their withered souls a little. Why, I suppose everybody needs love, even the police who clamp down on prostitutes need love; evil people are evil only because nobody has ever shown them a bit of love. Of course, this particular leopard is different from the one seventeen years ago, but even this one will be freed when the time comes. He, too, will see the light one day when the wall which surrounds him collapses, and the brightness which he's not yet able to see will illuminate him. Did our enchantingly beautiful one get her milk today?' he asked, thinking of the cat they had in the flat, and when Lakmé nodded without a word, Mr. Kopfrkingl smiled at the leopard for the last time. Then they slowly walked back towards the exit through the heavy, sweltering stench of animals from the dear, blessed spot outside the leopard's cage, where they had met seventeen years ago. Mr. Kopfrkingl glanced at the corner towards the snake, which was still watching the pink-faced girl in her black dress outside the cage, and said: 'It's strange that they've put a reptile with the predators, perhaps it's here only as a decoration or a complement . . .,' then he tenderly led Lakmé over the threshold onto the path bordered with shrubs, at which point Lakmé smiled and said:

'Yes, Roman, ask Mr. Strauss to come to the restaurant. But give him the *correct* name of the restaurant, so that he won't have to search for it.'

And Mr. Kopfrkingl halted there, in the faint early spring breeze, which had stirred his hair, there on the path bordered with shrubs, and nodded kindly. His soul was at peace, as is the case with people who have just held a service before the altar. He looked up at the clear, sunny sky, stretching far and wide. He gazed at it for a while, and then raised his hand and pointed vaguely at it as though drawing attention to the stars, not visible in daylight, or to a magnificent picture or an apparition. . . . And next Sunday at noon . . .

Next Sunday at noon, during the lunch he was buying at the Silver Casket, Mr. Kopfrkingl said to a small, stoutish gentleman who had a good-natured look about him:

'Mr. Strauss, did you have to look for this restaurant?' And when Mr. Strauss, the small, stoutish gentleman, shook his head good-naturedly, Mr. Kopfrkingl gave a sigh of relief, and Lakmé, so it seemed, did likewise. I'm so glad that you haven't been looking for the restaurant,' said Mr. Kopfrkingl, 'you know, if one says The Boa . . .' Mr. Kopfrkingl glanced fleetingly at the signboard of the restaurant by that name, behind the tree-tops, 'if one says The Boa, it's quite clear. Everybody knows beforehand what to expect from a boa. Why, its very name indicates it, I suppose, unless it's a tame and trained one. Not long ago I read in the papers about a trained boa which was able to do sums; *divide by three*. But a silver casket is a mystery. Nobody knows until the last moment what such a casket might contain until it's completely opened and examined . . . well, Mr. Strauss, I've a little, modest proposal.'

Mr. Strauss, the small, stoutish gentleman, smiled unassumingly at Lakmé, the blackhaired beauty, and at Zina, who was also blackhaired and beautiful. He obviously derived pleasure from their beauty; they were sitting at the table in a graceful, indeed tender manner, if it is at all possible to sit tenderly. He smiled at Milivoj too, who was also blackhaired and good-looking, but probably still somewhat dull; he was sitting and gaping a bit. Mr. Kopfrkingl joyfully called for the waiter to bring more drinks and sweets.

The sun shone from the tree-tops onto the table on that warm, early spring Sunday at noon. The Boa, otherwise The

Silver Casket, was, in fact, an open-air restaurant. Even a band played there, and in the front there was a parquet floor on which one could dance. Into the sunshine breaking through the trees on this early spring Sunday the waiter brought drinks and sweets. Mr. Strauss and Zina had a glass of wine, Lakmé had tea. 'You know, Mr. Strauss,' smiled Mr. Kopfrkingl glancing at an adjacent tree where a small notice hung on a hook: *Drapes and Curtains repaired by Josefa Brouček, Prague-Hloubětín, 7 Kateřinská Street,* 'you know, Mr. Strauss, my dear one comes from a German family really, from Slatiňany, and in her home they used to drink tea, she likes tea . . .' Mili took a lemonade and a sweet. 'Mili likes sweets, Mr. Strauss,' smiled Mr. Kopfrkingl and glanced again at the small notice with Josefa Brouček's advert on the adjacent tree. 'Milli is particularly fond of choc-ice, he has a sweet-tooth, the little brute.' Then he looked at his hand with its pretty wedding ring, which rested alongside a small cup of coffee, and said: 'And I'm abstemious. I don't drink. I don't drink, and if I do, then only a drop, just symbolically. Nor do I like cigarettes. I didn't even get used to them in the war when we were fighting for Austria. I don't like alcohol or nicotine. I'm abstemious.' Mr. Kopfrkingl had a sip of coffee, and glanced at the bandstand where the musicians were taking their seats. At a table near the parquet floor he caught a glimpse of an *elderly woman in spectacles* with a foaming glass of beer beside her and said:

'Well, Mr. Strauss, you're a commercial traveller in confectionery. You're in regular contact with shop-assistants and shopkeepers and that in itself must be an extremely pleasant job. People who deal in confectionery must be gentle, kind, good. You know, Mr. Strauss, I can't help it, but I feel quite sorry for them. What if you offered those nice people something else beside your firm's goods? It's not the sweets I'm concerned about, but they themselves, those gentle, kind, good people . . . But have no fear,' he gave a quick smile, 'no insurance companies, no insurance policies, but something entirely different. While you are offering them sweets, you could dive into your brief-case again and take out application forms for the crematorium. Five crowns commission for every subscriber to cremation.'

The band began to play some lively music, clarinets and fiddles struck up, the double-bass as well, and three couples went onto the dance floor. One of the couples consisted of a *little old fat man in a stiff white collar with a red bow tie* with a very young, pink-faced girl in her black dress. The little man grabbed her back and began to circle with her on the same spot as though he were in a cage. Sitting at the table near the dance floor was the elderly woman in spectacles with the foaming glass of beer beside her; she was shaking her head with a bitter smile. Then she blew the foam to the ground and took a swig.

'You know, Mr. Strauss,' Mr. Kopfrkingl smiled at the table, lit by the sun behind the tree-tops, 'God arranged it very well for people. The fact that some suffer, that's something else. Animals suffer too. At home I have a splendid book in yellow cloth. *It is a book about Tibet*, about Tibetan monasteries, about their highest ruler, the Dalai Lama, about their fascinating faith. It reads like the Bible. Suffering is an evil we are supposed to eliminate or alleviate at least, to *shorten*. But people commit evil because they're surrounded by a wall which prevents them from seeing the light. However, God arranged it well. He did well when he said to man 'Remember that dust you are and to dust you shall return.' He did a good thing when he formed man from dust, but mercifully granted him the opportunity to turn into dust again. After all the hardships and torments life brings, after all the disappointments and imperfections of love . . .' He glanced at the elderly woman in spectacles with the glass of beer beside her, sitting by the dance floor, 'God granted in his mercy man the chance to turn to dust again.

(12)

A crematorium, Mr. Strauss, is greatly pleasing to God. Why, it helps him to *accelerate* the transformation of man into dust. Just imagine, if man were formed from some flame-proof material. If he were, well ...' Mr. Kopfrkingl shrugged his shoulders looking at the elderly woman in spectacles with her glass of beer beside her, 'then you'd be welcome to put him under ground. Fortunately, he's not flame-proof. Do you know how long it takes before man turns to dust in the ground? Twenty years, but even then the skeleton does not disintegrate completely. In the crematorium it takes a mere seventy-five minutes even with the skeleton, now that they have installed gas instead of coke. People sometimes object that Jesus Christ was not cremated but buried in the ground. Well, Mr. Strauss,' said Mr. Kopfrkingl with a smile, 'that was something else. I always tell those nice people: the Saviour was embalmed, wrapped in linen, and buried in a tomb cut in the rock. Nobody's going to bury you in a cave, nor embalm nor wrap you in linen ... Arguments, Mr. Strauss, like the one that the coffin will split under the weight of the soil, and how painful it would be should the earth fall on the head, such arguments, of course, won't stand up. Why, when a person is ...,' Mr. Kopfrkingl gave a nod, 'dead, he no longer feels it ... But there is another reason for cremation. Look, Mr. Strauss, if people didn't have themselves cremated but were buried in the ground, what would the furnaces be for?' After a moment of silence, Mr. Kopfrkingl glanced towards the dance floor and said:

'We live in a good, humanitarian state which builds and furnishes crematoria ... for what? For no earthly reason? So that people visit them like museums? Why, the sooner man returns to dust, the sooner he'll be liberated, trans-formed, enlightened, be reincarnated. Besides, the same applies to animals. There are countries, Mr. Strauss, where it is the custom to cremate animals after death: in Tibet for example. That book of ours about Tibet is amazing,'

Mr. Kopfrkingl glanced at the tree where the notice 'Drapes and Curtains repaired by Josefa Brouček, Prague-Hloubětín, 7 Kateřinská Street' hung on the hook, and added: I had no idea that there's a Kateřinská Street in Hloubětín. I only know the Kateřinská Street in Prague II.'

The band finished playing. The clarinets and fiddles fell silent, the double-bass as well, and the couples left the parquet floor. The little old fat man in the stiff white collar with the red bow tie left with the pink-faced girl in her black dress, and the elderly woman in spectacles nearby took a swig. Mr. Kopfrkingl called the waiter, paid and everybody got up.

'You're fond of music, Mr. Strauss,' said Mr. Kopfrkingl with a smile as they were leaving The Boa, otherwise The Silver Casket, Restaurant. 'Sensitive people love music. Wretched and poor are those, I once read, who die without having learnt the beauty of Schubert or — Liszt. Are you, by any chance, related to Johann or Richard Strauss, the immortal creator of "Der Rosenkavalier" and "Till Eulen-spiegel"?'

'Unfortunately not, Mr. Kopfrkingl,' said Mr. Strauss good-naturedly, looking at the restaurant's signboard, un-der which the pink-faced girl in her black dress was talking to a young man and the elderly woman in spectacles was slowly approaching them from the direction of the tree. 'I'm not, but I like Strauss's music. Not because of the name, though,' he smiled, 'I'd probably like it even if my name was Wagner, for example. Which way would you like to go . . .'

'We're not going home yet,' said Mr. Kopfrkingl with a kind smile, 'it's an early spring Sunday, and I'd like my fam-ily to have a bit of fun. I'd like *to refresh them a bit, divert their thoughts, so I'm taking my dear ones* to Madame Tus-saud's . . .' he gave a smile.

'Oh, Madame Tussaud,' said Mr. Strauss.

'Of course,' said Mr. Kopfrkingl apologetically, 'it's not the real Madame Tussaud. It's just a tawdry sort of imitation, but what do I care? It's better to see a commonplace, tawdry imitation than nothing. *It is*,' he said and pointed beyond the trees and shrubs, 'over there . . . Mr. Strauss, how glad I am . . .'

'A nice, witty fellow,' said Lakmé after Mr. Strauss had taken his leave with a polite word of thanks. They were then walking slowly to Madame Tussaud's under the trees and shrubs in the sunny afternoon of an early spring Sunday. 'If you think that it will be worthwhile . . .'

'It will, my dear,' smiled Mr. Kopfrkingl, 'I get fifteen crowns for every subscriber, but I can't go round and see people like a pedlar. I work long hours. Sometimes I have a lot of duties in the evening. Where would I get time for the children, for you . . .? Mr. Strauss has far more opportunities in going round the confectionery shops. He can kill two birds with one stone. I'm only sorry I offered him one third of the commission and not half. I wouldn't like to cheat him. I wouldn't like to be like that trained boa which was able to divide by three, but no longer by two. Indeed, my dears, you have no idea,' he said, 'what Mr. Strauss has been through already. First some evil person deprived him of his position as porter in the porter's lodge. He retired. He was there because there was something wrong with his liver,' he smiled sadly at Zina who was walking by their side, 'this is sad, indeed. Our Mr. Vrána, our watchman from the lodge in the courtyard, has got something wrong with his liver as well, and that's why he's there. Then Mr. Strauss lost his wife, she died of *consumption of the throat,*' he smiled sadly at Lakmé, 'then he lost his son, he died *of scarlet fever,*' he smiled at Mili, who was walking slowly behind them. 'What hasn't he gone through already! Actually, I'm surprised that he hasn't gone mad yet. Well, he's survived everything, thank God. And I'm going to increase his commission on the grounds

(15)

that he's successful,' Mr. Kopfrkingl said resolutely. 'I'm sure he's going to be successful.'

'Yes,' Lakmé gave a nod, 'he's certainly a good business-man. He's Jewish.'

'Do you think so, my dear?' smiled Mr. Kopfrkingl. 'I don't know. His name doesn't prove it. Strausses are not Jewish. Strauss means ostrich.'

'Names do not mean anything,' smiled Lakmé, 'after all, you know yourself how they can be changed. You yourself call The Boa The Silver Casket: lucky that Mr. Strauss didn't look for it . . . You call me Lakmé instead of Marie and you want me to call you Roman instead of Karel.'

'That's because I'm a romantic and I love beauty, my dear,' Mr. Kopfrkingl smiled at his darkhaired beauty and took her tenderly by the arm, smiling at Zina at the same time.

'I didn't know,' said Zina, 'that people would be sitting outside under the trees at the restaurant already. After all, spring hasn't come yet. I didn't know either that you can dance there at lunchtime. I thought you could only dance at 5 o'clock tea parties and in the evening.'

'People dance in the middle of the day at The Silver Casket, and people already sit outside because it's warm,' said Mr. Kopfrkingl glancing at the trees and shrubs under which they were walking. Then he turned round to look at Milivoj who was still walking slowly behind them, and added with a tender smile:

'So that we can have a bit of fun for once, refresh our-selves a bit and divert our thoughts . . . We're here already.'

They had just reached a tent with a wooden box-office and a coloured signboard which said:

WAXWORK A LA MADAME TUSSAUD
THE GREAT PESTILENCE – BLACK DEATH
IN PRAGUE 1680.

II

In the wooden box-office by the tent sat a little old fat man in a stiff white collar with a red bow tie. He was selling tickets. The entrance to the tent was covered by a fringed, red curtain, and a small group of people was standing in front of it, apparently waiting to be let in. Mr. Kopfrkingl bought the tickets at the wooden box-office and then joined the group with his dear ones.

'Is it going to be something dreadful?' asked Mili uncertainly, gazing at the tent, at the painted skeletons on the side and at the entrance with the fringed, red curtain, and Mr. Kopfrkingl nodded his head sadly.

'Suffering,' he said to the boy quietly, 'but suffering against which man is armed nowadays. You're not going to be frightened, are you?' he said. 'After all, it's just a tawdry sort of imitation.'

A hand with large sparkling rings emerged from behind the fringed, red curtain. For a while it rested motionless on the red cloth with fingers spread as though making a parade of them. It then drew the curtain aside and an elderly, dark-skinned woman in a shiny red-green-blue dress with large earrings and beads made her appearance. She looked like an old American Indian or Greek woman and mispronounced her "rs" a little.

'Would you like to come in, ladies and gentlemen,' she sang out, bowing deeply, 'children as well. The show has much to tell.'

'It's probably the proprietress,' Mr. Kopfrkingl told Lakmé and tenderly asked her to go into the tent.

They found themselves with the other spectators in a kind of enclosure which was apparently meant to be an apothecary's shop. In the weak yellow light there hung a coat-of-arms with a coiled snake. Around them were painted shelves, chests of drawers and cupboards with earthenware jugs, flasks of pewter and tin, gilded boxes, kegs with small bags, and on the counter there was a gigantic book, scales, basins, pans, funnels and sieves. Behind the counter stood a bearded old man with long hair. He had a black coat trimmed with threadbare fur and a beret. He had rosy cheeks, sky-blue eyes and pearl-white teeth in his slightly opened mouth. He was holding scales with something in them. By the window a woman in a smock and apron was bending over a mortar, squinting slightly at the spectators. In front of the counter stood two middle-aged men. One of them, very beautifully dressed with gloves and a hat adorned with a long feather, was watching the apothecary weighing his goods. The other one, in a black, shabby hood and frock, was holding a coin in his hand and gazing towards the woman by the window. At the back among the shelves there was a kind of niche, covered by a net curtain, behind which the contours of a motionless shadow could be seen.

'Ladies and gentlemen, what you are about to behold are terrible things,' said the proprietress rapidly, mispronouncing her "rs". 'It is the year 1680 and Prague is being swept by dreadful tidings; there's no escape for the human race from the dread Black Death which people face, blasted by its breath. An ominous conjunction of the stars has occurred and poisoned wells were common. Nature moved and evildoers heard, forgetting they were human. Misfortune looms large over Prague — alas for the city. We are now in the apothecary's shop on the Old Town Square – oh, the pity.' Then she went on, mispronouncing her "rs":

'On the shelves and in the cupboards you can see spices for various pains and diseases. Here you can observe cinnamon, nutmeg, saffron and a keg of pepper.' The proprietress pointed to the bowls, jars, jugs, and the rings on her fingers sparkled. 'And here are sweet-flag, ginger, sulphur and the tooth of the wether. Over there is white sugar, brown sugar, Venetian soap and caraway seed. Here are rubber, petroleum, fennel and bottles of mead. Here you can observe dried frogs, eyes of crayfish, wolf's liver, elephant's ivory, chicken entrails and skins. Here in this box are pearls, rubies, beads, alabaster, alum, carnelian and dragon's fins. Here in the cupboard are oils, dried herbs, barks of trees, snails' shells and bread of St. John,' she pointed to the cupboard. 'Here are amulets, vinegar, camphor and fur of the fawn. Here are ointments for wounds and sores, here traps for boars. Here bones from the heart of deer can be seen, here rosemary is turning green. Here's jellyfish and its flipper, here-' she pointed to the woman by the window, 'the apothecary's wife in her jacket and apron is pounding juniper. Here is dog's, cat's, stork's, rabbit's and hare's grease which cures many a disease. Here's snake's dripping, which children find appetizing. Here in this jar are human fats, so soothing and bland, and here hangs a piece of a thief s dried hand. On the counter there are six scales symbolizing celestial trials.' The proprietress paused for a moment, perhaps to catch her breath, for she spoke rather quickly. Then she pointed to the bearded man with the long hair, rosy cheeks, blue eyes and white teeth, and said:

'And now, ladies and gentlemen, observe the apothecary. He is holding the scales, weighing the rosemary, rue, aloe pills, remedies and fumigants for people to ward off their ills. And here are the customers.' She pointed to the two figures in front of the counter. 'They are looking for some medicament to save themselves from a terrible predicament. The first one, in gloves, red-black velvet, top-boots and *a hat with a long feather*,' she indicated the figure, 'is the Town Clerk, held in reverence and esteem, scanning the six scales with a curious gleam. He came to our shop in a crisis and is going to buy the spices, then off to the barber-surgeon in haste, for bloodletting is to his taste. The other one beside him, in the black hood and frock,' she indicated the figure, 'is the Rat-catcher. To escape from the plague on baths he relies; the town of vermin he cleans and purifies.

And there is somebody – spying, prying,' she pointed to the shadow, the contours of which could be seen behind the net curtain in the niche, and cried out: 'Light!' Light was projected onto the curtain and the shadow changed into a boy with long fair hair, in a green pointed cap, leather vest and red-yellow trousers. In one hand he was holding scales and the other he held up with forefinger raised. He looked like a figure on a poster advertising coffee. The proprietress bowed deeply and said: 'This is our dear good elf by the name of Ralph who can see everything. Misfortune looms large over Prague — alas for the city – with the Clerk and the Rat-catcher now we're leaving the shop in the Old Town Square — oh, the pity. You can see everything life-like. Put out the light!' The lights in the apothecary's shop went out, the display plunged into darkness. Somewhere at the back several quick steps could be heard on the boards, as if somebody was jumping about, and the proprietress pointed to another curtain and sang out: 'Would you, please, come here, ladies and gentlemen, children as well? The show has much more to tell.'

'That was really life-like,' said a woman visitor with *a long feather in her hat* and a string of beads around her neck.

'They're wax figures,' the stoutish man accompanying her in a bowler hat and carrying a stick, growled ill-humouredly, 'they're figures made of wax, that's obvious.'

Mr. Kopfrkingl took hold of Lakmé by the arm and with the others they entered the next enclosure.

This was a room full of books, bowls, basins, kettles, gallipots, funnels, burners and retorts. On the table there was a globe with a ring around it and a skull, but it was not an apothecary's shop. Sitting behind the table was a bearded old man, but he did not look like the apothecary. He had a silk blouse and a beret with golden braid. He was not as pink as the apothecary, but paler, and a bit seedy or worried. His eyes were not as blue nor his teeth as white.

His hand, which was grazed, was holding a cupping glass and a knife. On the wall there hung a faded picture with two triangles, stars, comets and a multitude of lines and marks. Standing further off, half-naked, were the Town Clerk and the Rat-catcher. They were twisted and distorted, paler and yellower than in the apothecary's shop with somewhat protruding eyes. They were almost horrifying. Behind the window with the net curtain illuminated in blue, the light contours of a motionless shadow could be seen.

'Yes, ladies and gentlemen,' cried out the proprietress, 'this is our Town Clerk and Rat-catcher, two people struck down by the plague. They are covered with tumours and blains, under the arms, behind the ears they feel the pains. The Black Death moves on at a swift pace, bodies roll, there's no escape for the human race, the bells toll. They applied juniper oil, but will they be rewarded for their toil? They fumigated their homes with frankincense and rose-mary, burned pine-wood, ate grated elephant's ivory, pearls, rubies, all this did not help, their bodies hurt, the plague has crippled them for good. They pray, fast, repent, bewail, all to no avail, and thus were forced to see the physician without fail. Ladies and gentlemen, we are now visiting the physi-cian in the Old Town on the Italian Square further down ...'

'This is just like a stage-show,' said the woman visitor with the long feather in her hat, watching the display in excitement. The fat man in the bowler hat with the stick gave her a push.

'This is no theatre,' he said bad temperedly but with assurance, 'this is a waxworks. Everything is made of wax,' he made a sharp movement with his hand.

Mr. Kopfrkingl smiled at Lakmé, Zina and Mili, who was watching it all, agape, and said:

'What would the good doctor Bettelheim from our apart-ments say to all this if he saw it? He would know how to deal with it today. He would.'

'Ladies and gentlemen,' the proprietress went on quickly, mispronouncing her "rs", 'behold how death came about, so people believed in those times, as they waited on the plague in those dreadful climes. Learned books taught that it was because of an ominous conjunction of the stars and poisoned wells, that it was Nature's and poisoners' work. The physician examined the Town Clerk and Rat-catcher, told them to smell myrtle, rue, marjoram carefully, then to go to the baths and there wash themselves in rose-water, camphor and vinegar thoroughly. Then to fumigate their dwellings, to pray and fast, for it stops the infection and the plague at last. To eat lemons and all things sour, for they weaken the Black Death's power. With this knife,' the proprietress pointed to the small knife the physician held in his hand, and the rings on her fingers flashed, 'the physician will draw blood from the poor patients in a gentle flood. Now — there behind the window like a living being – Light!' she cried out and light illuminated the blue window with the net curtain where the shadow turned into the boy in his cap, vest and trousers, 'Ralph our elf, is grinning. He is observing, watching everything, measuring time in a sand-glass.' Bowing deeply she pointed to the boy's hands in which he was now holding a sand-glass, while looking like a poster figure advertising tea. 'He measures time in his hour-glass to find when death's rage will pass. And where will the two go when they leave the surgery? Into the baths for full recovery! Would you, please, follow me, ladies and gentlemen, children as well? The show has more to tell. Put out the light,' she clapped her hands. The light in the physician's surgery went out. In the darkness at the back quick steps and jumps could be heard, and the group approached another curtain.

'Into the baths!' cried the woman visitor with the feather in her hat to the people around her, 'I wonder if there's going to be water and steam as well?'

'Don't be daft,' snapped the fat man accompanying her, giving her a push, 'just watch it and shut up. You're not in a wash-house. You're in a waxworks. Everything is wax here.'

They went through the curtain and found themselves in a small room with wooden wash-basins, wash-tubs, vats, baths and buckets. Sitting in the baths were two figures: the Town Clerk and Rat-catcher. They were now deathly pale, had slightly open mouths and were staring at the spectators with their eyes very wide open. They were truly horrifying. Sticking out of the tub was a woman's head, with her eyes turned up to the ceiling as though she were praying. A pink-faced youth was bending slightly over behind the tub and washing the woman's hair with a brush. Standing by the window was a fat woman in a smock, apron and bonnet, with a bucket in her hand. In twilight behind the net curtain the contours of a shadow could be seen, it was obviously the boy, Ralph, the elf. He was standing astride, pointing to the people in the baths with his arms stretched sideways, and laughing like a figure on a poster advertising soap.

'The baths,' Mr. Kopfrkingl smiled at Lakmé, Zina and Mili, 'the old baths. How much more magnificent is the bathroom in our flat. That beautiful, delightful bathroom of ours with the mirror, bath, ventilator and the butterfly on the wall.' He gave a smile.

'We are now in the St. Francis' Baths close by the Rat-catcher's dwelling,' said the proprietress quickly, mispronouncing her "rs". 'The customers come here to purify their bodies and ease their swelling. This fellow is,' she indicated the youth behind the woman's head in the tub, 'a servant, bath-keeper and underling, he's also a barber, barber-surgeon and hireling. His grandfather was a wax-chandler, who made candles of wax and wore shoes of Spanish leather to relax. His father was a grinder who sharpened knives, made pots, had long whiskers and saved lives. This woman in the jacket, apron and pinafore with the bucket is the bath-woman, laundress and seamstress, she was also many a man's mistress. The woman in the tub committed adultery, and so was put in the pillory. Now in great fear she cleans herself here. And there in the baths you will have recognized our unfortunate Town Clerk and Rat-catcher, who have just left their medical adviser. They are now bathing in rose-water, vinegar and camphor, and no longer wish to be held in honour. And who is there in the window and able to see everything? Light!' cried out the proprietress. After the light had illuminated the boy standing astride behind the net curtain, pointing to the people in the baths and laughing, she bowed deeply and said: 'This is our elf, the best of all. He is grinning like a living being. He would like to help the unfortunates, the *good* one, if only he wasn't so *poor*. And now behold, ladies and gentlemen, life is approaching its end; it is not on the mend. Keep close to me constantly, we are leaving here presently. Put out the light,' she clapped her hands. The display in the baths was plunged into darkness. At the back quick steps and jumps could be heard ... and they all went on through another curtain.

They found themselves in complete darkness, but only for a while.

Suddenly light blazed down from the ceiling. Several women in the audience screamed, the woman visitor with the feather in her hat cried out 'How dreadful!' Smiling sadly, Mr. Kopfrkingl took a firm hold of Lakmé and turned slightly to look at Zina and Mili. Facing the spectators, *the Rat-catcher was hanging from a hook* with a black net in the background. He had a black hood and *frock*; his hands and legs sagged in the air, and his face with its protruding tongue and bulging eyes was yellow. The rope on which he hung swayed a little. 'Yes,' cried out the proprietress flashing the rings on her fingers. 'Our unfortunate Rat-catcher hanged himself. He was a man of deeds, the pestilence he no longer heeds. He didn't want to suffer, torture himself, infect others thoughtlessly, so he put an end to his life abruptly. His dead body hangs on the rope, for him there is no hope.'

'He's life-like,' the woman visitor shook her head in excitement, her feather trembling in the air, 'life-like.' The fat man heaved a sigh and growled furiously: 'He's dead, see! He hanged himself, you heard that. We're in the waxworks, it's made of wax.'

'They took him down,' said the proprietress quickly, *mispronouncing her "rs"*, 'buried him on the outskirts of the town in a public grave in St. Roch's Churchyard. They poured lime over the plague-pit, they did their part. Light!' she cried. The light illuminated the boy in profile against a dark net in the background. He was standing there in his cap, blouse and trousers, with one of his legs thrust forward as though he were about to start marching, and in his hand he held a stick with a little cross. He looked like a figure on a poster advertising quality shoes or trousers. 'Our dear elf buries people,' said the proprietress bowing deeply, 'his face is full of redness, sadness and gentleness. He would like to help the poor wretches, if only he was not so penniless. He can't romp and gambol about like your children every day, no man can have luck always at play. He doesn't even have any shoes . . . Ladies and gentlemen, follow me through to see what more death can do . . .' And the proprietress approached another curtain. The figure hanging from the rope and the boy disappeared in darkness. Somewhere in the back on the boards quick steps and jumps could be heard . . . The spectators approached the curtain, and the woman with the feather exclaimed to the group:

'"What more death can do?" This is going to be something still more horrible, I'm trembling all over. What's the noise that's always there at the back when it's dark? As if somebody was jumping about. Look out!' she said to the fat man with the stick, 'your hat is going to fall off.'

'Shut up. You're crazy,' the fat man snapped at her. 'You behave as if you were at some executioner's. Who'd jump about back there? You're in the waxworks! Well,' he bellowed at her, 'who'd jump about on the boards back there? Everything is made of wax in here. Get a move on . . .' He gave her a push and adjusted his bowler hat. They found themselves in a new area.

This was a kind of corridor or hall, or even a cellar, with the door covered by the net curtain. There were tiles on the floor, black tables and chests, and among them . . . among them, stood the Town Clerk in the hat with the long feather and high boots, twisted and pale and *clenching in his hands a sort of rod or stick which he raised threateningly over a small girl, who was about to sink onto one knee, desperately shielding her head and face.*

'There you are, I knew it. It's the mortuary,' the woman visitor cried and the feather in her hat quivered. The fat man with the stick shook his head furiously and gave her a push.

'You don't know a damned thing,' he wheezed furiously. 'You're an idiot. This is no mortuary, this is the waxworks. Everything is wax here. I'm telling you for the hundredth and last time. Look at it and stop jabbering, or . . .' he raised his stick.

'That, ladies and gentlemen, as you are aware, is the Town Clerk,' the proprietress said quickly, mispronouncing her "rs", and the rings on her fingers, and her beads and earrings sparkled. 'This is quite beyond belief, not even a beast would seek such a relief. The unfortunate Clerk stands with legs astride holding the stick. To stop the girl spreading plague, he intends to beat her to death, to make her yield up her last breath. No longer the devil's helpmate, but liberated from the evil spirit, she can go to heaven as a woman of merit. Will the Town Clerk be successful or is life to be the girl's lot? I am sure you all wish health and joy to the poor wretches who rot. So let our happy good elf with the name of Ralph reveal himself – Light!' the lady of the waxworks clapped her hands bowing deeply. 'Light, I say! . . .' she gave another cry for only a click could be heard, and the light did not come on. But then it did. She gave another deep bow, and the boy, behind the net curtain on the door, revealed himself to the spectators. He was smiling archly with his head on one side and one leg slightly bent, with a child's balloon resting by it. He was shaking his fist at the Clerk and holding a bowl painted in gay colours in his other hand. He looked like a colourful figure on a poster from the toy shop.

'Ladies and gentlemen, you have seen the terrible blows of the pestilence in Prague in 1680,' said the proprietress, mispronouncing her "rs", 'The Black Death, ruining people's health. What you are to see next are bones from St. Roch's Church where death delights in the plague victims, be they rich or poor. But before you view the bones in meditation, you'll be glad to learn if Ralph is going to be the girl's salvation. Ladies and gentlemen, now comes the culmination, the good fairy will reveal herself in exultation and with a magic spell will free the elf from his hell. She is going to give life to the elf, the wax puppet. A poor wretch, he cannot romp and gambol like your children every day. He lives from hand to mouth, no man can have luck always at play, he doesn't even have any shoes . . . you'll see a live and happy puppet if, for our plague victims, you contribute to the packet. Those who are virtuous are always illustrious —' The lady of the waxworks approached the boy, raised her bejewelled hand over him and sang out:

'Abracadabra, don't be mad, dear Ralph, come alive, be glad. Ask our dear kind guests to give a few coins for our sad wretches in their nests. Ask them too to give you some coins for your little coat and shoes. The guests will give quite gladly, so that you can play in the sun rejoicing madly.' The lady of the waxworks gave a deep bow and touched the boy's cap with her finger. Several women in the audience screamed. The wax figure of the boy blinked, stirred its lips, moved and came alive. Bowing and smiling the boy held out the coloured bowl . . .

'So it's not a waxworks after all,' the woman visitor with the feather shouted at the fat man with the stick while clutching at her beads, 'it's you who were jabbering about it being all of wax. Look, he's moving. What's in that brain of yours? Oh, my God, he's got the balloon. It makes me feel quite odd!'

There was a rattling sound in the fat man's throat; suddenly he raised his stick; the woman visitor screamed, clutched at her beads and fled through the curtain. Full of rage, the fat man said, apologetically, to the others: 'She's probably gone mad, she's an idiot. She does it to me all the time. I'd better not take her out anywhere anymore.'

The lady of the waxworks quickly thanked the guests for their contributions, wished them a pleasant journey and drew the curtain aside so they could go into the last compartment. Standing against a background of black paper were a number of miserable human skeletons and on the floor lay a broken string of beads and a feather.

'What's happened to the woman?' Mili blurted out. 'Has she run away?'

'She has,' said Mr. Kopfrkingl, glancing sadly at the skeletons. 'It was probably a shock to her.'

'Is the boy, the elf, employed here?' asked Mili.

'He's probably the grandson of the proprietress,' Mr. Kopfrkingl gave a nod.

'Poor woman,' said Mr. Kopfrkingl after they had stepped out of the tent into the fresh Sunday afternoon, and turned to look around a little. Standing in front of the tent was the fat man with the stick, holding his hat in his hand and furiously wiping his forehead with a handkerchief. 'Poor woman, but perhaps it won't be anything serious. It was just a waxworks after all, just a tawdry sort of attraction. Modern science will cure her. It would be enough for the good philanthropist from our apartments, Dr. Bettelheim, to have a look at her; she would be cured. Have you ever seen Dr. Bettelheim's surgery, my dear?' he smiled at Lakmé. 'He invited me there once. He's got a beautiful old picture on the wall in there, but it doesn't matter . . . It's terrible indeed what people went through in those days. They were helpless against the plague, but those were the Middle Ages.'

'Middle Ages, my dear Roman,' said Lakmé when they had stepped out onto the street. 'People suffer nowadays too. Once they suffered from the plague, today from something else.'

'Yes,' Mr. Kopfrkingl gave a nod, 'today they suffer from hunger, poverty, exploitation, various persecutions and catch new diseases which were not known then – leprosy for example. When I think of Mr. Strauss again, or even of some people *from our place*,' Mr. Kopfrkingl looked down at the ground, 'what bitter lives they've had. Though it's true that all these hardships are only temporary. One day everybody will free himself, break away from hardships, be reincarnated . . . Why, those who died from the plague in those days, escaped their suffering too –,' Mr. Kopfrkingl glanced at the window display in a pink confectionery shop they were just passing. 'They've been dead, transformed, for a long time now, but what's the use! This will happen to us all one day. The problem is how to suffer as little as possible now, while each of us is living his only life. It's exactly as it's written in our beautiful book about Tibet.' Then he said:

'In the Middle Ages they used to bury their dead in a public grave, she meant the common one, and they sprinkled lime over the bodies to stop the infection from spreading! How much wiser it would be if they had cremated them. There'd be no chance of infection, and the tortured bodies of the poor wretches would be transformed into ashes much sooner . . . How happy I am, my dear,' Mr. Kopfrkingl smiled at Lakmé, 'to be able to provide you with a better place to live in than they had at that time. At least we've a hall, a living-room with the piano, a dining-room with the radio, the bathroom, if nothing else. Well, things may get better what with the good Mr. Strauss and all that. I'll give him half the commission on some pretext or other.' Mr. Kopfrkingl smiled kindly at Zina who was walking by their side. And then he turned round to look at Mili who was now walking a long way behind them, he'd probably taken a look at a window display, possibly of the pink confectionery shop they had passed a while ago. Mr. Kopfrkingl stopped, Lakmé and Zina did likewise, to wait for Mili, and when Mili reached them at last he said:

'Well, Mili, how is Dr. Bettelheim's nephew, Jan? And the Prachař boy, Vojta, from the third floor? Well?' he asked kindly, and without hearing Mili's answer, he said:

'Don't stray so far behind, Mili. Hurry up.'

III

'I've bought some pictures for you, my heavenly one,' said Mr. Kopfrkingl to his wife, not long after their visit to the waxworks. They were in their wondrous dining-room, which contained, among other things, a bookcase, a cabinet, a standard lamp, a small mirror and a radio. 'Pictures from the first of our additional income. To make our home even more magnificent.'

'And have you sent the commission to Mr. Strauss yet?' asked Lakmé.

'Yes, of course I have,' he said, moved by her meticulousness. 'I gave him not one third, as I promised at the Silver Casket, but one half, straight away. I didn't even wait to hear just how successful he would be. By doing this I dispelled any idea that I would cheat him. I expect he was pleasantly surprised. Are the children at home?'

'Zina is having her piano lesson, and Mili is with Jan Bettelheim.'

'I'm very glad to hear that,' smiled Mr. Kopfrkingl. 'Jan Bettelheim is a nice, tidy boy, and if Mili is with him, it can only mean that he's somewhere nearby. Jan goes only as far as the bridge. He also does well at school, and is fond of music. Madame goes to operas with him often ... He neither drinks nor smokes ... Well yes, my dear ...' Mr. Kopfrkingl gave a smile when Lakmé glanced up at him in surprise, 'you shouldn't be surprised. The fact that he's only just turned fourteen like Mili doesn't matter in the least. Take Vojta Prachař from the third floor. He's fifteen, and I feel almost sorry for his father.' When Lakmé again glanced up at him in surprise, he said, slightly embarrassed:

'It's not for us to weigh and judge others. We shouldn't be suspicious. Each of us, even though abstemious like me, has enough faults of his own. I don't really mean it like that, but Mrs. Prachař complained to me on the stairs yesterday that her husband drinks.' And then, glancing at the package, he continued:

'That unfortunately her husband drinks more and more. Should it go on like this, she said, her husband will become a confirmed alcoholic. Zina was there and heard it, unfortunately. I'm very sorry about that, and I feel sorry for Mr. Prachař, and even more for her, Mrs. Prachař, and their Vojta. I fear the boy could take after his father. There are tendencies people inherit in a family. I'm afraid that Vojta Prachař already smokes, and that he's inclined to stray about like our Mili. God knows from whom Mili inherited this tendency. Not from me, nor from you. Neither of us has ever wandered about. When I recall that *Suchdol* case ... But I know,' he added tenderly and swiftly when Lakmé gave him a reproachful glance. 'I know Mili's not inclined to alcohol or cigarettes, thank God. He's a sensitive lad, and if he's with Jan Bettelheim, I'm glad. He can have gone only as far as the bridge.' Then he said:

'As far as Mr. Prachař is concerned, I must persuade Zina not to talk about it anywhere, particularly not in front of Vojta. That boy might be shattered by such a picture of his father. But now, my dear,' Mr. Kopfrkingl gave a smile, 'we're going to hang up the presents. Before I unwrap the pictures, allow me to tell you how I came by them.' Mr. Kopfrkingl took the scissors out of the cabinet to cut the string with which the package containing the pictures was tied, and said:

'It was like this. On the way from the post office it occurred to me to buy something to add to our flat. Even though we have a beautiful flat we mustn't be lax in maintaining it. We must constantly improve its appearance, as our aunt from Slatiňany would say, that kind soul who's almost a saint by now. And besides, various business acquaintances may come here from now on. In the course of time I intend to find somebody else apart from Mr. Strauss, but that's neither here nor there. Well, on the way from the post office,' said Mr. Kopfrkingl, untying the string, 'I called on Mr. Holý, the picture-framer, on Nekázanka Street. You probably don't know him, for I only saw him for the first time in my life today . . . He's a lonely old fellow, a widower; his wife, he told me, died eight years ago in the Virgin Hospital. He has a daughter; when I entered the shop she was measuring frames at the counter, she looked very nice. She's such a pretty pink-faced young girl in a pretty black dress . . . Mr. Holý had nothing but common birches, lilacs and red poppies,' said Mr. Kopfrkingl, untying the string. 'In short, scarcely anything except for one single picture, but it was the one he wanted to frame at that very moment; the frames his little girl was measuring were meant for that very picture. These pictures,' Mr. Kopfrkingl pointed to the package, 'were standing in the corner. He didn't really mean to sell them, he probably just wanted to frame them. They're two prints, he gave me them both for eight crowns, the good one . . .' and with a smile Mr. Kopfrkingl unwrapped the pictures. On one of them was a town with a hill, a castle, a church and mountains in the background.

'I thought,' Mr. Kopfrkingl smiled at his wife, 'that it was Salzburg or Ljubljana. The towns are as alike as two true brothers; both of them have a hill in their midst, a church-roof, mountains in the background – after all I know both of them from the war – but it's actually Maryborough, the capital of Queen's County in Ireland, named after Queen Mary. It has ruins of a castle from 1560, a court house and a lunatic asylum. Where are we going to hang it?'

'In the bathroom?' Lakmé gave a smile and he was touched. In fact, he thought the bathroom the most beautiful room in the flat and he liked it best.

They went into the bathroom with the Maryborough picture. The room was indeed beautiful. There was a big mirror, a wash-basin, a bath; a pretty ventilator, with a cord suspended from a hook, shone white on the wall near the ceiling. Below the ventilator a large yellow butterfly was stuck on a pin under glass in a black frame.

'You know, my dear,' Mr. Kopfrkingl gave a smile, 'I do indeed think the bathroom the most beautiful room of all, and I love it, but my dear, flowers or a nude would be rather more suitable here. Not Maryborough. Considering that people make linen in Maryborough,' he gave a smile, 'we'll hang the picture in the hall by the coat-rack. Over those pretty shelves for shoes . . . And the second picture,' he said when they returned to the dining-room, 'is a portrait. A perfect print of a perfect gentleman. He's Louis Marin, professor at the Collège des Sciences Sociales, who later became "rapporteur général" for the budget and a Deputy. In Poincaré's government he was Minister of Pensions . . .'

'But there's a different name here,' Lakmé stooped down to look at the mount and then glanced up at her husband questioningly.

'Of course,' he stroked her black hair, 'he's a Nicaraguan President, Emilian Chamorro, from 1916. But that doesn't matter, my dear. He'll be Louis Marin. We'll cover up the name on the mount with a strip of paper. A beautiful exotic face can adorn the dining-room. A fellow enjoys his food more when he can see noble faces while eating. We'll put it . . .' Mr. Kopfrkingl looked round the walls of the dining-room a little, and then he said: 'We'll put it here by the window. Here by that dear gentle wall chart of ours by the window. The picture Mr. Holy's pink-faced daughter in black was measuring frames for would be more suitable for our dear gentle wall chart; it was a *wedding* procession. Still, I can always call on Mr. Holý sometimes and buy it. Then we'll hang Marin somewhere else,' he said and straightened slightly the dear gentle wall chart which was hanging on a black cord by the window.

'Father, you've bought pictures,' said Zina when she returned from her piano lesson a while later, and Mr. Kopfrkingl stroked her hair and cheek and said:

'I bought the pictures from the first of our additional income, my beautiful one. I bought them to make our flat even more magnificent, so that we're not lax in maintaining it, as our saint from Slatiňany would say,' he smiled a little sadly at Zina and Lakmé. 'It's our home.' And then he asked:

'How did your piano lesson go today, Zina dear?'

'Oh yes, yes,' Zina heaved a sigh glancing towards the window at the exotic face by the chart, 'I had to repeat the étude. The old trout nearly rapped my fingers with her little stick.'

'But Zina, my little one, don't talk like that,' said Mr. Kopfrkingl kindly. 'Don't call your teacher "the old trout". She's an elderly lady. When you are her age and a sixteen-year-old little girl calls you "the old trout", you won't like it either. Women are touchy about it, particularly beautiful ones, my beauty. We mustn't harm anybody, even in thought. Zina,' said Mr. Kopfrkingl earnestly, 'please, don't tell anybody what you heard Mrs. Prachař say about her husband. Don't let on you know anything, especially not in front of Vojta. It might upset him a great deal. Actually, I'm surprised that Mrs. Prachař complained like that in public . . .' and when Zina quietly nodded her consent, Mr. Kopfrkingl stroked her and said to Lakmé:

'My heavenly one, the children could drop in at our aunt's in Slatiňany sometimes, take her some flowers, beautiful white lilies for example. They would at least have a bit of rest. How sorry I am, Lakmé, that your late mother can no longer be with us; how well she could cook, bake . . .' Then he smiled at the cat in the corner of the dining-room and went to see if her dish was full of milk. The cat ate in the dining-room.

'Yesterday or whenever was it,' said Mr. Kopfrkingl gazing down at the cat's dish, 'I read that they'd arrested a woman who was selling skinned rabbits in the market. They were in fact cats. Poverty drove the poor woman to these swindles. Although we live in a good humanitarian state, we haven't been able to get rid of poverty entirely.'

Then Zina lightly arranged her hair in front of the small mirror in the dining-room. Mr. Kopfrkingl went to tidy up the things in the bookcase where he fondly straightened his most beloved yellow book about Tibet. Then he glanced at the cabinet, the standard lamp and the radio, and after that he went to help Lakmé make sandwiches. The Reinkes were to come in the evening.

The Reinkes belonged to the Kopfrkingls' circle of old friends, though they did not meet often over the years.

They were stout, elegant people. Willi had a grey suit with a blue tie and a green hunting hat with a braid, and his wife a well-tended coiffure and biggish earrings. Lakmé served wine; they all toasted each other. Mr. Kopfrkingl and Lakmé only wetted their lips, Zina took a longer sip, about the same as Mrs. Reinke. Then Mr. Kopfrkingl asked his guests to partake of the sandwiches and salted almonds. Mrs. Reinke put a sandwich on her cut-glass plate; Willi also helped himself to a sandwich, and at almost the same moment took a newspaper out of his pocket and handed it to his friend Kopfrkingl *with its frontpage uppermost.*

'Married men live longer . . .' read Mr. Kopfrkingl when *he turned over the inside pages,* 'according to the statistics. We're well off, Willi, we have our dear ladies to thank for that. If it were not for them we'd die earlier.' And while they all laughed Mr. Kopfrkingl looked for another tasteful piece of news to read out. 'Here,' he said, and the smile on his face faded a little.

'"Man wrecked on the rocks of life lives in pigsty. At the parish's expense . . ." and here: "Banger explodes in boy's mouth. The eight-year-old . . ." Our Mili should hear that,' Mr. Kopfrkingl gave a sigh. 'Although he's fourteen he likes straying about all the time. I'm not sure whether you know about it, you haven't been here for such a long time.' Mr. Kopfrkingl glanced at Willi and Mrs. Reinke. 'On one occasion, he didn't even come home, we had to have the police search for him. They found him in the field near Suchdol at night, he wanted to spend the night in a haystack. It was summertime. He's not at home now. Is he still outside?' he smiled at Lakmé.

'He's gone with Jan Bettelheim, only as far as the bridge at most,' she said.

'Bettelheim?' Willi looked up. 'A strange name. Isn't that the doctor with a nameplate downstairs?' And after a nod from Mr. Kopfrkingl, he got up and went to the window and glanced at the wall chart hanging there on its black cord, Mr. Kopfrkingl watching him a little uncertainly.

		I.	II.
1	8.00– 8.30	8.30– 9.45	
2	8.30– 9.00		9.00–10.15
3	9.00– 9.30	9.45–11.00	
4	9.30–10.00		10.15–11.30
5	10.00–10.30	11.00–12.15	
6	10.30–11.00		11.30–12.45
7	14.00–14.30	14.30–15.45	
8	14.30–15.00		15.00–16.15
9	15.00–15.30	15.45–17.00	
10	15.30–16.00		16.15–17.30

Willi glanced at the wall chart, and then glanced in silence at the exotic picture hanging beside it.

'Who on earth's that, Karl? An ancestor of yours?'

'That's the former French Minister of Pensions, Louis Marin,' said Mr. Kopfrkingl, slightly embarrassed. 'I bought it at Mr. Holý's on Nekázanka Street today. Mr. Holý has a picture-framing shop. He's a lonely old fellow, a widower; his wife died eight years ago at the Virgin Hospital. He lives with his daughter, she's such a pretty pink-faced young girl in a pretty black dress . . . There's another picture from Mr. Holý hanging in the hall, Maryborough. That's a town in Ireland, named after Queen Mary who founded it in 1560. But Mr. Holý has a picture which would be more suitable for the wall chart here, a wedding procession. Oh well, Willi,' said Mr. Kopfrkingl somewhat more calmly once Willi had taken his seat again, 'when I remember how we went to the War, sang "Heil dir im Siegeskranz" and "In der Heimat, in der Heimat" in front of the railway station in Prague, fought on the front, died . . . but war goes against my grain, I don't like it. War causes much more suffering to people than civilian life. It brings poverty, the break-up of families, ruined marriages, blood, pain, destruction, and not only to people. When I remember what the poor horses had to go through as well in such a military campaign . . . There should be peace, justice and happiness in the world.'

'That's not going to come out of the blue,' said Willi, 'we have to fight for it. Wishes and speeches are good for nothing, only deeds matter. And they can be carried out only by people who are one hundred percent.' Then he said:

'The just settlement of Europe lies in *their* hands, not in the hands of inferior weaklings. Look at Austria,' he took the newspaper and turned it front page uppermost. 'Her annexation to the Reich constitutes the first step. Hitler is an ingenious politician who rids a nation of one hundred million people of its hardships, poverty, unemployment, secures them a just position in the world . . . Didn't you see the leaflets published by the SdP? The Sudeten German Party?'

'But I was under the impression', said Mr. Kopfrkingl, surprised, 'that you're a member of the Agrarian Party!'

'Of course,' said Willi, 'but of a German one. A merger with the SdP was agreed in January. I can in all modesty say that I had a certain part in the merger. A united German front is being formed in Czechoslovakia. Wrong was done our nation after the war and we have to make it good. All of us who have German blood, and who fought against the German enemy in the war, want peace and are rallying to the banner of the SdP. There's still time, the leaflet says. It's the party's sort of application form . . . join the party. Without Hitler we'd be at rock bottom.' Mr. Kopfrkingl was gazing at Willi in embarrassment, and then he said:

'Have some almonds.'

Mrs. Reinke gave Mr. Kopfrkingl a rather hard glance, took the newspaper, turned over the pages and read:

'"Man wrecked on the rocks of life lives in pigsty. Banger explodes in boy's mouth . . ." What other *important* news have we got here . . .' she continued turning over the pages. 'Ah, here: "He fell into boiling water. In Berehovo at the silver wedding anniversary. . ."'

Mr. Kopfrkingl was now gazing at Mrs. Reinke and said kindly: 'These are tragedies, Erna. Mr. Strauss was pensioned off by an evil fellow from the porter's lodge. Then his wife died of consumption of the throat and his son of scarlet fever. Now he's an agent in confectionery and even sells people application forms for the crematorium . . . Or that recent case,' he said, 'of the woman whom they arrested because, out of poverty and hunger, she was selling cats instead of rabbits. Although we live in a decent humanitarian state, we haven't been able to get rid of poverty entirely. Or women,' he said, 'who suddenly suffer a shock . . . Not long ago we saw such a case with our own eyes . . . when they look at the plague, for example,' he said, gazing at Mrs. Reinke, 'in the waxworks for example. Have some almonds,' he said to Mrs. Reinke.

'I don't know about that SdP,' Lakmé, embarrassed and, taken aback, took a sip of the tea which was standing beside the wine bottle on the table. 'After all, the children go to Czech schools, only Czech is spoken at home, just like now . . .'

'We've never spoken German here,' agreed Mr. Kopfrkingl. 'I also have nothing but Czech books . . . Our German blood, why, it's but a drop.'

'A drop,' Willi gave a rather harsh laugh and glanced at his friend Kopfrkingl, 'a drop. But a fellow with conscience and a heart feels even that drop. If it were not for Hitler, we would, I repeat, be at rock bottom. We'd perish of unemployment, we'd peg out from hunger, they'd bury us like dogs. *That* is tragedy,' Willi said with emphasis. 'The nation is what matters here. Not one or two people, some women who sold cats or went mad in some waxworks. Here one hundred million people suffer and endure hardship! You can't see the wood because of one stupid splinter in your eye. Because a Mr. Strauss was sacked from the porter's lodge, you don't see the *whole!*'

Willi glanced at his watch and said that he had another appointment with Boehrmann in the German Casino at eight o'clock. 'He's a key man in the SdP and is going to Berlin to consult with Reichsminister Goebbels,' he said rather drily. 'This republic stands in the way of our salvation. But I'd have to expound it to you at length,' he said to his friend Kopfrkingl. 'It would be a long exposition, and Erna and I must be going now. If we didn't have a car in front of the house we would be too late.'

The Reinke couple rose and at that very moment somebody rang the bell. Zina rushed to open the door and soon Mili timidly entered the dining-room. As he came through the door he was taking off his beret with both hands.

'Where've you been, Mili,' Willi gave him a pat on the back. 'With Jan Bettelheim? At the bridge?'

'Just in front of the house,' the boy blurted out, 'we were watching the cars.'

'Mili likes cars,' said Zina.

'He has a strange theory,' Lakmé gave a smile. 'He divides cars into coloured ones and green and white ones. Coloured cars are all civilian, Dr. Bettelheim's car and yours for example . . . green cars are military and prison vans, and white cars . . .'

'And white cars are celestial,' smiled Mr. Kopfrkingl, though a little disconcerted. 'Celestial for angels.'

The Reinke couple gave a laugh, Willi took his green hunting hat with the braid, then they took their leave and went.

'Willi was never an inferior weakling,' Mr. Kopfrkingl then said to his darkhaired beauty by the window under the wall chart on the black cord and the picture of the Minister of Pensions. 'He has always been a one hundred-percent fellow. Now he has a car in front of the house and a high office in the Henlein party. Did you hear, Mili?' he said to his son, who was tucking into the almonds by the table. 'A pity you weren't here. It was interesting, the nice conversation we had here. Mr. Reinke had to go to the grammar school at first, like you, before he took over the chemical factory. He didn't wander about, the police never had to search for him, as they did for you, and look. He has an appointment with a Mr. Boehrmann who's going to Berlin to see Reichsminister Goebbels. He's got a car in front of the house, and you *lag behind* in German. We speak Czech here, without doubt, and I don't like Willi's politicking in the least, let alone his contacts with the SdP, but, my dear boy, you ought to know German, at least for yourself. There's nothing else for it. It is a nation of one hundred million people. Jan Bettelheim knows German, I'm sure, and Vojta Prachař attends some lessons.'

'But there are some people who don't know it either,' said Mili. 'That one from the waxworks for example, that grandson, Ralph . . .'

'But,' Mr. Kopfrkingl gave a surprised laugh, if it is at all possible to give a surprised laugh, 'why, that's something else. He doesn't need it,' he gave a laugh. 'He travels to fairs.' Then Mr. Kopfrkingl said:

'We'll switch on the radio, there's a nice concert on. How is our enchantingly beautiful one?' he asked, going to look at the cat's dish in the corner for the second time that evening, and then he said:

'Zina, my dear! Look, don't let the animal suffer so. Why, the bowl's nearly empty . . . Ah, Liszt's Preludes . . .' he said as the radio began to play, and he tenderly stroked the cat.

Today was Friday and the old woman, on seeing Mr. Kopfrkingl approaching her, was already nodding her head.
She stood there every Friday morning and Saturday afternoon, even when it rained and when it snowed in winter.
But now as it was summer, she didn't so much as have a
headscarf and looked like one of the grey Fates from a fairy
tale. Mr. Kopfrkingl gave her a twenty-heller coin and went
in to the porter's lodge in the courtyard. He glanced at
the framed schedule for the day; there were five men and
five women, a thirty-year-old Mrs. Strunný among them.
Mr. Kopfrkingl exchanged greetings with Mr. Vrána, who
had a liver-complaint and was making tea in the porter's
lodge, then walked slowly towards the building through
the empty courtyard. For fifteen years I have been going
past Mr. Vrána and his porter's lodge into the Temple of
Death, he thought, looking in turn at the paving stones on
the ground and the crystal-clear sky above the building.
For fifteen years I've been coming here like this, and I'm
still seized by the same sacred feeling. It's something like
my marriage. For seventeen years I've been with Lakmé, he
glanced at his hand with its wedding ring, and she excites
me in the same way as she did on the first day we met in
the zoo near the leopard. Happy human love. How poor
are those who never get to know it . . . Then he entered
the building where Mr. Fenek was sitting in the second
porter's lodge. Mr. Fenek was an old, careworn eccentric
with a long nail on his little finger. Behind the porter's
lodge he had a small room with a sofa, a cabinet and a
chair. As Mr. Kopfrkingl went past him, Mr. Fenek bent his
head down and his hands, holding the newspaper, which
he was probably reading before, trembled. Mr. Kopfrkingl
gave a smile and a nod. Then he went through part of the
corridor and entered the cloakroom. Beran and Zajíc were
already in their overalls.

'You've already read about it,' said Zajíc. 'The English are urging us to give way to Henlein's supporters. Imagine them and the French delivering us to the tender mercies of the Germans. I'm so worried . . .'

'We won't give in to them,' said Beran fiercely. Beran was rather fierce. 'They will declare a state of emergency in the borderland.'

With a smile, Mr. Kopfrkingl took out his snack and the book about Tibet he was in the habit of reading during breaks.

'Don't be afraid, Jozef,' he said kindly to Zajíc. 'What would they leave us to the mercy of the Germans for? Everything is going to be alright. I'm saying it although I have a drop of German blood myself, and even my dear one is German through her deceased mother from Slatiňany. You can't blame anybody for his origins; after all, I don't care. I'm not interested in politics,' he said to Beran. 'For me it's enough to see that there's no poverty, no injustice and that nobody suffers unnecessarily. Unfortunately, things are not yet quite as they should be. Oh, Mr. Dvořák,' he now noticed a youth, standing quietly by the coat-rack in the corner of the cloakroom. 'Don't you worry, Mr. Dvořák. You look as if you are suffering from stage fright. But never mind, Mr. Dvořák, I'll instruct you as considerately as I possibly can. Would you like to come with us too, Mrs. Liška?' He gave a smile in the direction of the mirror where Mrs. Liška, a young cleaning woman, was knotting her headscarf; she was getting ready to go home. 'No? Why, you don't really know how the mechanisms and automatic processes in this place work. Mrs. Podzimek knows.'

'Mrs. Podzimek has been here for fifteen years, Mr. Kopfrkingl, and I don't have to know in order to clean the corridors,' said Mrs. Liška rather dejectedly, and finished knotting her headscarf. Mr. Kopfrkingl, gazing at her with interest, holding the snack and the Tibetan book, gave a smile and thought: What can be the matter with Mrs. Liška, with her speaking so dejectedly? It's so nice outside and she is wearing a headscarf. Why, the old woman outside in front of the courtyard doesn't have one. Then he thought: I've never been in a steam bakery, yet these furnaces of ours always look to me like ovens for baking our daily bread . . . After Mrs. Liška had left, Mr. Kopfrkingl changed into over-alls and then nodded towards the coat-rack in the corner where Mr. Dvořák was still standing quietly.

'Fancy you taking it up, Mr. Dvořák,' Mr. Kopfrkingl gave a smile. 'You are, so it seems, still very young. You've proba-bly just finished your training. But we all started like that, Mr. Dvořák, even Mr Beran and Mr. Zajíc. Chin up and have no fear. Poverty, envy and gossip apart, fear is mankind's greatest enemy. If mankind could rid itself of fear, it would live much more happily. Fear doesn't even permit us to enjoy the beauty of Nature which is all around us. Well, let's go.'

They stepped out into the corridor and Mr. Dvořák asked timidly whether he could smoke.

'Of course,' nodded Mr. Kopfrkingl, 'why shouldn't you? We're not in a cinema nor in a hospital, here we're in the midst of fire. Have your cigarette, if it'll do you good, Mr. Dvořák. No thank you,' he refused the offered cigarette in a kind manner. 'I don't smoke. I don't drink either, I'm ab-stemious. But if you think that a drink will help you, just go on and have one. We who are abstemious must be sensible and understanding,' smiled Mr. Kopfrkingl kindly, and then he began to expound the Temple of Death to Mr. Dvořák.

'This loudspeaker,' he said, pointing to the loudspeaker, black against white tiles, 'is here for us to hear the proceed-ings inside the funeral hall, Mr. Dvořák; you'll hear beautiful speeches and sublime music. Are you fond of music, Mr. Dvořák?' he asked, and when the youth, dropping the ash from his cigarette onto the palm of his hand, nodded, Mr. Kopfrkingl said: 'That's good, Mr. Dvořák. Sensitive people love music, as a rule. Poor are those who die without having learnt the beauty of Schubert or Liszt. Are you, by any chance, one of Antonín Dvořák's kin, the author of "The Devil and Kate", "The Cunning Peasant", "Rusalka". . .' and when Mr. Dvořák shook his head, Mr. Kopfrkingl said apologetically: 'You're often going to hear Dvořák's Largo from "The New World", Fibich's "Poem", "Shine, Golden Sun", and "My beautiful Czech Lands, my Czech Lands" here . . . So this is the loudspeaker. This button,' Mr. Kopfrkingl pointed to the button on the white tile, 'opens the iron curtain of the funeral hall and lets people out into the ether. But under the new director, we only open it occasionally. Mr. Pelikán upstairs opens it for us, as a rule. Mr. Pelikán and the director are decent people, we get on well with them. Mrs. Podzimek cleans up for them . . . And now look at this wall chart,' said Mr. Kopfrkingl and, together with Mr. Dvořák, approached the wall on which the wall chart was hanging on a black silk cord.

		I.	II.
1	8.00– 8.30	8.30– 9.45	–
2	8.30– 9.00		9.00–10.15
3	9.00– 9.30	9.45–11.00	
4	9.30–10.00		10.15–11.30
5	10.00–10.30	11.00–12.15	
6	10.30–11.00		11.30–12.45
7	14.00–14.30	14.30–15.45	
8	14.30–15.00		15.00–16.15
9	15.00–15.30	15.45–17.00	
10	15.30–16.00		16.15–17.30

'It probably seems complicated to you,' Mr. Kopfrkingl gave a smile, 'but it only appears so. In reality, it's very simple.

The first service begins,' he pointed to the first column of figures and the wedding ring on his hand flashed, 'at eight o'clock. Every service lasts half an hour. There are two furnaces, and now that they've installed gas instead of coke, the complete transformation of the deceased into ashes lasts one hour and fifteen minutes. Thus it can be calculated that the first two coffins disappear into the furnace immediately after the service, after the curtain has been opened, and you can see it,' he pointed to the figures, 'in those figures too. But the third coffin,' he pointed to the third line, 'has to wait on the dead-end track for fifteen minutes because there's no room for it in the first furnace yet, and the fifth and sixth even have to wait for thirty minutes, as you can see here . . . At lunchtime we have about a one-hour break. When the weather is fine, you can take a stroll in the cemetery. If you go out *the back way*, you'll arrive at the Vinohrady cemetery on leaving ours. You don't even have to go past Mr. Vrána's porter's lodge in the courtyard. If there are four funerals in the afternoon, we get out to the open air at six,' Mr. Kopfrkingl pointed to the ceiling as if pointing to the sky. He gazed upwards for a while as if seeing the stars. Then he smiled at Dvořák, who was looking dejectedly at the wall chart, smoking and dropping the ash into the palm of his hand, and went on:

'Don't worry about the wall chart, Mr. Dvořák. It's our sort of schedule, a sort of timetable of death. Why, it is, in fact, the most sublime timetable in existence in the world. A timetable nobody can escape unless he has himself buried in the ground. There the timetable is slightly different, less perfect, *longer,* because it depends on underground water and living creatures, and not on mechanics. This one,' he pointed to the wall chart, 'could embellish a royal chamber or the palace of the ruler of the Himalayas . . . Well, and now this,' Mr. Kopfrkingl approached the furnace. 'What you see here are two thermometers. The first one,' Mr. Kopfrkingl pointed to the first thermometer, 'indicates the temperature of the air leaving the recuperator; that's a machine in which the hot gases are changed into pure, red-hot air. That's to say, Mr. Dvořák, cremation is done with hot air; neither the coffin nor the body must come into contact with flames, that's important. There's even a kind of law about it. Laws, Mr. Dvořák,' Mr. Kopfrkingl gave a kind smile, 'are here to protect people . . . The second one,' he pointed to the second thermometer, and the wedding ring on his hand flashed, 'registers the temperature right inside, in the furnace. It should be over 950 degrees. We maintain it at one thousand degrees, and this is good for checking it. The permissible maximum is 1020 degrees. If you exceed the limit, then the bones will turn into a glassy black substance and there will be no ashes. That would be a great disaster, Mr. Dvořák,' said Mr. Kopfrkingl. 'The purpose of this whole mechanism is to turn man into dust, for him to return quietly and quickly to where he came from. At around one thousand degrees the bones remain dazzlingly white, and as you fill the urn they will disintegrate into ashes, and this is how it should be. We check the correct course of the process with the aid of these thermometers, but there are other ways too. We go up onto this little scaffold,' Mr. Kopfrkingl pointed to a sort of scaffold, 'and look into the furnace through that little window in the opening up there. It's of non-fusible smoked glass, Mr. Dvořák. It's the most sacred window in the world, Mr. Dvořák. If you look through it you'll see straight into the kitchen of death, into the workshop of God Himself, when the soul departs from the body and flies up into the ether. However, there's no need for you to look just yet. We'll do it for you. Well, and now I'll tell you what happens when the deceased has been transformed.' Then Mr. Kopfrkingl took a few steps and said:

'After the deceased has been transformed, his ashes will be put into those tin cylinders. They are rather narrow – a kind of container. They are 23 cm high and 16 cm in diameter and are standardized. There's even some kind of law about that. But the soul will not go in there,' Mr. Kopfrkingl gave a smile. 'It does not come into being to end up in a tin container but in the ether. Rid of the fetters of suffering, liberated, enlightened, it is subject to laws other than those of these tin cylinders; it wanders into another body. Well, and what else is there to say?' Mr. Kopfrkingl smiled encouragingly at Dvořák. 'What else? Perhaps the fact that there's a direct entrance into the furnace from the outside, from the funeral hall, along the tracks, even that dead-end one. The opening for the coffin or, as we call it, the inlet, measures one meter twenty by one meter twenty; this is standardized as well. A fellow could only pass through it comfortably if he *bent* a little *but nobody does so* . . . Come, Mr. Dvořák, while we're at it, I'll show you one more thing, the preparation room . . .' Mr. Kopfrkingl beckoned kindly to Mr. Dvořák, who stubbed out his cigarette, and led him along the corridor to doors further off, behind the furnace and the tin cylinders.

'So this is the preparation room, Mr. Dvořák,' Mr. Kopfrkingl opened the door. 'Mrs. Liška cleans up here. It looks a bit like a cellar or a corridor. There are tiles on the floor. In the corner over there, behind that net curtain, is a kind of niche. Only some sort of advertising poster's hanging there, nothing else . . . Well, and here on these tables are coffins. They are, as you can see, open, and have numbers and names on them. That's to avoid any mix-up. There are five of them just now, the morning batch. The sixth coffin, in fact the one that goes first into the funeral hall at eight o'clock, is already in the viewing room for the mourners to take their farewells. But what's more important, Mr. Dvořák,' said Mr. Kopfrkingl and gave a smile, 'not every coffin goes into the viewing room. There are coffins,' Mr. Kopfrkingl gave a smile, 'which go directly from here into the funeral hall, either because the mourners don't want to see them, or because they cannot be shown, as death by infection was involved, or the body is no longer in a state fit to be displayed. *These coffins, Mr. Dvořák, are already nailed down for good.* This is case number three today . . .' Mr. Kopfrkingl pointed to a nailed coffin, bearing the number three and the name of Osvald Řezníček, and then looked round quickly. In the corner by the niche with the curtain he saw an iron rod, wanted to say something about it to Mr. Dvořák, but then he fixed his eyes on the fifth coffin. 'We're laying Mrs. Strunný to rest in the fifth coffin today,' he said and beckoned to Mr. Dvořák to come nearer. There was an incredibly beautiful woman in the coffin.

'I've already seen her, yesterday,' said Mr. Kopfrkingl with slightly downcast eyes, while Mr. Dvořák stood somewhere behind him and peered into the coffin, frightfully pale. 'She doesn't have the pale, hollow cheeks, nor the protruding nose and cheekbones, as is usual with the dead when they breathe their last and when they're starved. Yes, Mr. Dvořák, starved,' Mr. Kopfrkingl gave a nod. '*Starvation* is the consequence of death. Neither does her skin look as if it was made of wax, like those figures in the waxworks for example,' Mr. Kopfrkingl pointed to it gently and the wedding ring on his finger flashed. 'Her skin is pink and her eyes cast down as though she were asleep. She looks as though she might wake and get up at any moment.'

'Perhaps you're thinking "what if she's not dead",' said Mr. Kopfrkingl after a while, seeing Mr. Dvořák staring. 'That would be the wrong idea, Mr. Dvořák. She has been pronounced dead, and in such a case it's our duty to cremate her after the service. To pronounce somebody dead is not only the most responsible, but also the most sublime official act carried out in this world. It is a decisive act, and we carry out our duties precisely. So you've seen these mechanisms and automatic processes of ours, Mr. Dvořák, and that's all for the time being, Mr. Dvořák.'

At ten o'clock, when Mrs. Strunný's service was beginning, Mr. Kopfrkingl said to Mr. Dvořák, who was smoking again:

'That woman was pronounced dead, and that settles it. It is something like passing a bill. Laws are here to serve people, and we must therefore hold them in reverence. We can only do her one last favour, to grant her another thirty minutes after the service on the dead-end track. She's fifth, and I'm happy about it, Mr. Dvořák. But in seventy-five minutes all that will remain of her will be a white-hot skeleton, and even that will disintegrate,' he said with a glance at the loudspeaker. 'In seventy-five minutes she'll be transformed into the matter she came from, into dust. In the ground it would take twenty years, and the bones would remain into the bargain. However, should Mrs. Strunný have been alive, it would have been a great misfortune for her. A misfortune because her life was before her. It would not be a misfortune,' said Mr. Kopfrkingl smiling at Mr. Dvořák, 'had she suffered a great deal in her life. There are such cases and, unfortunately, there are plenty of them. Suffering is evil and we ought to do everything in our power to alleviate it at least, or to *shorten* . . . But don't worry, Mr. Dvořák,' Mr. Kopfrkingl gave a smile, 'Mrs. Strunný was indeed dead, such mistakes no longer happen nowadays.'

Mr. Kopfrkingl then followed the service from the funeral hall through the loudspeaker, the second movement from Schubert's "Unfinished". Of course, the beauty in the coffin was hardly thirty. Then he opened the iron curtain in the hall with the aid of the button, and took the beauty onto the dead-end track. In the first furnace, Mr. Vlk had not yet been completely transformed; he still had those thirty minutes to go. Now and then Mr. Kopfrkingl read the book about Tibet, and the Dalai Lama, his faith, his reincarnation. Now and then he watched the thermometer for Mr. Vlk, to avoid exceeding 1020 degrees. At one moment he recalled what his friend Willi said when he and Erna visited them not long ago, and what Beran and Zajíc were saying today about the political situation. He listened to a speech from another funeral about what is one human life . . . then Mr. Holý's daughter flashed through his brain, the pretty pink-faced young girl in her black dress, measuring frames for the picture of the wedding procession in the picture-framing shop on Nekázanka Street. Then he thought of the young Mrs. Liška, who came to clean up here, and who was sort of dejected today . . . Then it was ten-thirty, and, with a sad smile he took the beauty's coffin into the first furnace.

'Ah well, Jozef,' he said not only to Zajíc, but also to Dvořák, who was staring in silence and was obviously still out of sorts, 'a while ago I listened to a speech from the funeral about what is one human life, and I thought of Mr. Holý's daughter, measuring frames in the picture-framing shop on Nekázanka Street, of our Mrs. Liška, who cleans up here, and was sort of dejected today . . . the things death deprives us of. If only people were strong enough to conquer Nature! If only they could get rid of suffering.'

And he watched the thermometer of the first furnace carefully to make sure that the ashes produced were as pure and fine as possible.

V

Dr. Bettelheim lived with his beautiful elderly wife, his nephew, Jan, and their housekeeper, Anežka Zelený, above the Kopfrkingls. The old doctor's surgery was situated over the Kopfrkingls' dining-room, but he owned the adjoining flat as well.

If the ceilings in our house were thin, thought Mr. Kopfrkingl in the surgery, where he was sitting just at that moment, half-naked and slightly stooping, on a round white chair, if they were thin . . . But how could my good Lakmé

(51)

perceive through the ceiling that the footstep up here is mine? I come here after surgery hours when there's not a living soul in the good doctor's waiting-room. As a matter of fact, I don't actually come here. I go out into the street, to the confectioner's, to buy something sweet for my heavenly one; she likes it sometimes, but not nearly as much as Mili. And then, he thought, my good Lakmé has never been suspicious. Just like me she believes that our marriage is exemplary, and that not one single little cloud has passed over our marriage in the seventeen years of its existence. Our marriage, thought Mr. Kopfrkingl and glanced at the wedding ring on his finger, is as pure as the sky over the Temple of Death just at the moment when nobody is being cremated.

Dr. Bettelheim took Mr. Kopfrkingl's arm, and while he looked for a vein and then swabbed it with a piece of cotton wool, Mr. Kopfrkingl gazed from his chair at the doctor's table, where a stethoscope, a mirror for examining the mouth, and a round mirror for the forehead lay. Dr. Bettelheim had these mirrors, although he was not a laryngologist. Then he gazed at the corner with the white glass cabinet with flasks, test-tubes and medicine. There was a Bunsen burner next to it . . . But Mr. Kopfrkingl was really looking at a large darkened painting in a black frame which had been hanging in the surgery for years. A pale cavalier with fiery shining eyes, a dogged face and a well-kept little moustache under his nose, in dark red velvet trousers, dark brown shirt and with a small gold sword at his waist, was at that very moment dragging a beautiful woman, in fact, not really a woman, but a pink-faced young girl in a black dress who was scarcely more than a child, over the threshold of a dimly lit room into a dark corridor. The room from which he was dragging her in such an incensed manner was probably a bedroom, because in the background behind a transparent curtain, the shape of an ancient headboard, clear symbol of all bedrooms, could be seen. In the corridor, a majestic man with a beard streaked with grey, a little black cap and a pale face contorted with pain was about to jump on the cavalier. Mr. Kopfrkingl fixed his gaze mainly on the languid pink-faced girl, and tried in vain to understand what was, in fact, the meaning of the scene. Had the cavalier dragged the girl *into* the bedroom, Mr. Kopfrkingl kept saying whenever he looked at the picture, then it would be understandable; however, he was not dragging her into, but *from*, the bedroom, and that always seemed rather strange to him. His eyes were fixed on the pink-faced girl in her black dress, even when the doctor put the syringe on his arm; and he went on gazing when the doctor pricked his arm, drew the blood and then pressed the cotton wool on it. After that the doctor went into the corner with the white glass cabinet, injected the blood into a test-tube, then approached the adjoining burner, held the test-tube over the flame of the burner, at which point Mr. Kopfrkingl tore himself away from the picture. The doctor pronounced his verdict. 'Negative, Mr. Kopfrkingl, you're healthy.'

He had been saying it for a good many years, and every time it took a load off Mr. Kopfrkingl's mind. If one counted the loads over the years, thought Mr. Kopfrkingl, our dining-room ceiling would have had to collapse under their weight.

'Do you still think these tests necessary, Mr. Kopfrkingl?' said the doctor, putting his instruments away, and Mr. Kopfrkingl turned to the picture and nodded. I maintain, he thought inwardly and glanced at the wedding ring on his finger, that I do not associate with any other women except my heavenly one, but at the same time I'm afraid of being infected. I should not like to look like a fraud or a hypochondriac in the eyes of this kind doctor . . . And so he always told him that he was afraid of infection because he was employed in the crematorium.

'You know, Doctor,' he repeated, 'I keep saying that I don't associate with any other women except my heavenly one, but at the same time I worry whether I'm infected. I'm afraid that you may think me a fraud or a hypochondriac. I'm afraid of infection because I work in the crematorium.'

'But you don't come into contact with the dead,' the doctor told him, 'and after all, the fact is that such infection is impossible.'

'I know, Doctor,' Mr. Kopfrkingl kept answering him, 'but I'm sensitive. I would have to shoot myself if I found out that I'd infected my wife. I'm doing it to set my mind at rest.'

'I'm doing it to set my mind at rest,' Mr. Kopfrkingl repeated and again glanced at his wedding ring. 'It would be horrible if I found out that I'd infected my wife. I'm abstemious, I don't drink or smoke, and should I harm my wife in *such a way*, I'd have to shoot myself,' he said and recalled Mr. Prachař from the third floor who unfortunately drank, Mrs. Prachař, his wife, for whom he felt sorry, and their Vojta worrying that he might inherit the tendency to drink. Then he said quickly:

'Our Mili is always straying about, Doctor. God knows who he inherited it from, none of us has suffered from it. I'm worried that we'll have to have the police search for him as we did when he strayed into Suchdol and wanted to spend the night in a haystack. How glad I am, Doctor, that he's friends with your Jan. When he's with him, I know he's only gone as far as the bridge at most, or watches cars somewhere in front of the house. He plays such a strange game. He divides the cars into coloured, green and white ones. The green ones are military or prison-vans, and the white ones are ambulances, the Red Cross. I always say,' Mr. Kopfrkingl gave a smile, 'celestial cars, for angels. Your car is blue, that is, it's coloured,' Mr. Kopfrkingl gave a smile. 'I'm very glad indeed that he's friends with your Jan. Such wanderings are dangerous for boys nowadays.

In the borderland, as I've heard, they've declared a state of emergency. They say that there was a rally of National Socialists in Nuremberg, and Hitler gave a speech there. They say he spoke aggressively, against us . . . Who knows what is going to happen. Doctor, I'm worried . . .' he added and thought inwardly: I'm worried just like that Mr. Zajíc of ours and I'm almost afraid. It could mean hell for many people.

'Don't you worry now, Mr. Kopfrkingl,' smiled the doctor. 'Violence does not reward anybody for long. It can only last a short period, but it can't make history.'

And when Mr. Kopfrkingl gave a little sigh of relief, the doctor said:

'People do not tolerate violence for ever. You can stun, intimidate them, force them underground, but for how long . . .? After all, we live in a civilized world, in Europe in the twentieth century.' Then he said:

'Aggressors are defeated in the end, Mr. Kopfrkingl. Look at the borderland. The Czechoslovak government declared a state of emergency, and the whole Sudeten German putsch collapsed at once . . . You're looking at the picture,' the doctor gave a smile.

'I have been looking at it for years,' Mr. Kopfrkingl now gave a calm smile, 'and it still holds me in the same way as when I saw it for the first time. It excites me in the same way as it did years ago when I came to you for the first time . . .' And he thought, in the same way as my marriage with Lakmé or those feelings I have when I enter the Temple of Death. Strangely, time has no effect on my rapture whatsoever.

'What does the picture really signify, doctor?' he asked. 'Who is that beautiful pink-faced girl in the black dress . . . And then, I still don't understand the scene . . . that man is dragging the girl *from* the bedroom . . .'

'It would be a longish exposition,' the doctor gave a smile and seated himself behind the table. 'This picture is a family heirloom. We come from Hungary, and used to live in Pressburg, today's Bratislava. According to the legend, one of our ancestors in the eighteenth century – that's him, the one with the beard and the little black cap – had an unusually beautiful young wife, and the Hungarian count, Bethlén, wanted to abduct her. He resisted the abductor successfully. This is the very scene. It's the abduction. That's why the man's dragging her from the bedroom . . .' the doctor gave a smile.

'He saved her,' nodded Mr. Kopfrkingl. 'The abduction was not successful. . .'

'It was not successful,' nodded the doctor, 'that's the thing we were just talking about. Aggressors are defeated in the end.'

'It's obviously a masterpiece,' said Mr. Kopfrkingl appreciatively. 'Which painter . . .'

'He's not known,' the doctor shook his head, 'the painter didn't sign it. He obviously wanted to remain anonymous because he depicted Count Bethlén as an abductor and a Jew as a rescuer. We Bettelheims are Jewish, after all, Mr. Kopfrkingl. Well, we've always been rather persecuted, you know . . . The painter would have probably got into trouble for his approach then . . .'

While the doctor was filling in the health insurance certificate, Mr. Kopfrkingl gazed at the beauty in the picture. Now he understood the scene; the abduction which failed . . .

And suddenly he no longer knew who he felt more sorry for – the beautiful pink-faced girl, her old husband the rescuer, or the aristocratic abductor who was unsuccessful, but it was just a quick flash through his mind. He recalled Mrs. Strunný whom he had recently cremated, Mrs. Liška, the young cleaning woman, who had been slightly dejected these days, the daughter of Mr. Holý, the framer, the young pink-faced girl in the black dress . . . Mrs. Prachař, the wife of poor Mr. Prachař from the third floor, also flashed across his mind again. Then a number of other women he knew flashed across his mind; he glanced at the doctor.

'So here you are, Mr. Kopfrkingl,' the doctor gave him the health insurance certificate in a kindly manner. 'If you think it's necessary, come again. Your Mili,' said the doctor and rose, 'is a very nice boy. These wanderings about are nothing serious. Well, it's their age, you know. At that age boys like all kinds of romantic adventures; you have to expect it. When I was fifteen, I very much liked to follow soldiers when they marched past our place to the training ground behind Bratislava. But what about your wife, Mr. Kopfrkingl?' said the doctor. 'Sometimes she seems a little sad to me when I come across her. Is anything wrong with her . . .?' Mr. Kopfrkingl was almost speechless. He had never heard that Lakmé could be sad and that there was anything wrong with her. What is more, it had never in his life even occurred to him.

'There's nothing wrong with her,' he said, taken aback. 'It's the first time in my life I've heard anything like this. Nothing like this has even occurred to me so far . . . Does she seem sad to you, Doctor?'

'Never mind, never mind,' the doctor calmed him down quickly, seeing his astonishment. 'It was just my impression. I am mistaken, I'm sure. Come this way, Mr. Kopfrkingl,' he said and led Mr. Kopfrkingl through the door into the room. 'There's no need for Anežka to see you, she's washing the floor in the waiting-room.'

As Mr. Kopfrkingl was unlocking the door on the floor below with a little bag of pralines for Lakmé in his pocket, he shook his head inwardly and thought: The good Dr. Bettelheim thinks that Lakmé looks sad. My God, what does it mean? What's the matter with her? Is it really just an impression, a semblance? Why, I can't see anything the matter with her, perhaps I should ask her casually. And then he thought: Lucky that we have such a good doctor in the house. Lucky that he's such a philanthropist. Lucky that he always receives me after surgery hours, and so discreetly.

As he entered the hall he recalled what he had heard about violence and aggressors who are always defeated in the end, and about Jews who were *always* persecuted, and somehow the good doctor's two statements did not fit together. I also hear now and then, he recalled, that Hitler persecutes Jews in Germany. Why? After all, they are such kind and selfless people.

Then he took the little bag of pralines out of his pocket and entered his wondrous dining-room.

VI

The existing government resigned, and the one-eyed general became head of the new one. Then a general mobilization was announced. Life was in a complete whirl, though everything held together, raced ahead, flew forward, ready to land, engage and take up arms. A few days after the general mobilization had been announced, Mr. Fenek brought a peculiar object with him to the crematorium.

'See here, Mr. Kopfrkingl,' he wailed in the porter's lodge, thrusting a sort of glass box upon Mr. Kopfrkingl. 'Take a look. What you see are flies glued to these little squares of paper. These are called small fruit or vinegar flies, that is drosophilas, a two-winged insect, Mr. Kopfrkingl. They're being used in the study of genetics. This one, Mr. Kopfrkingl,' Mr. Fenek pointed with the long nail on his little finger, 'has two hundred species, and this one is called drosophila *funebris*. Would you like to have the box? I could let you have it very cheaply, Mr. Kopfrkingl. For a little bit . . .' Mr. Fenek lowered his voice, looking up with his tear-stained eyes, 'for a pinch of morphia . . .'

'It's an ornament,' said Mr. Kopfrkingl seriously, looking at the glass box. 'I appreciate flies like these, Mr. Fenek.

Once they were alive, buzzed, flew around. These were even used in the study of genetics, as you say, and now they're glued onto little pieces of paper. We have a butterfly pinned up in the bathroom. But,' he said then, 'where would I get morphia from, Mr. Fenek? Why, I don't even smoke,'

'But you have a friend who's a chemist . . .' wailed the eccentric.

'Mr. Reinke is not in Prague at the moment,' replied Mr. Kopfrkingl. 'The general mobilization has been announced. Everything's in a whirl, racing ahead, flying forward, ready to land . . . he's probably somewhere in the field . . .'

'Well, then you'll give it me when he gets back,' said Mr. Fenek, thrusting the glass box upon Mr. Kopfrkingl. 'I probably still have a little bit somewhere. Take it. Take it just for the sake of this funereal one . . .' he pointed to the black fly. 'Take it, Mr. Kopfrkingl . . .' and Mr. Kopfrkingl nodded, thanked him and took the glass box. The corridors smelled of lysol. Standing at the end of the corridor in front of the door to the preparation room was Mrs. Liška, her headscarf in her hand; she was about to leave. Beran and Zajíc had not yet arrived.

'I'm early today,' said Mr. Kopfrkingl to Mrs. Liška as he reached her with the glass box under his arm, 'because I wanted to see you.'

'There are better things for you to see,' she said uncertainly, knotting her headscarf by feel alone.

'You mean these disintegrating wretches?' Mr. Kopfrkingl cocked his head in the direction of the furnace at the back as he held the glass box under his arm and a briefcase in his hand. 'My dear, I'm an honourable fellow and I may well be moved by them. But you're alive. How long have you been living like this? You can't tell me that the meaning of your life is cleaning up here every morning. Getting up every morning, coming here and cleaning up, and then going back home. . . You know, Mrs. Liška, I've been thinking about you a lot in the last few days, even in the doctor's surgery.' Then he said:

'You know yourself how things are at present; the general mobilization has been announced. You ought to have somebody to belong to, somebody who'd protect you. You shouldn't be on your own like this. Let's meet tonight and talk about it. Have a bit of fun, refresh yourself, divert your thoughts,' he said, looking at her bare neck and drawing closer to her. She screamed, her eyes panic-stricken and broke into a slow run along the corridor, past the furnaces, towards the cloakroom. Mrs. Podzimek's voice could be heard from the front, asking what was going on.

'Murder in the crematorium,' called out Mr. Kopfrkingl with the glass box and the briefcase in his hand. 'I gave Mrs. Liška a fright.'

Mrs. Podzimek caught up with him. Mr. Kopfrkingl smiled at her, and she did the same.

'Mr. Kopfrkingl, you're making jokes and it's giving me the shivers. People shouldn't be joking in here, what with the furnaces and all that.'

'You're right,' Mr. Kopfrkingl gave a smile. 'But you yourself know I meant no harm, Mrs. Podzimek. Mrs. Liška is an attractive and lonely woman; she has nobody in this world. Times are hard, what with the mobilization. I wanted to talk to her a bit, chat to her, invite her out somewhere, to our place for example . . .' he said. 'She probably got a fright, poor thing. Well, perhaps I'll be able to invite her out some other time.'

'You know, Jozef,' he said to Zajíc while they were talking in the cloakroom about the mobilization and the Germans, looking simultaneously at Beran and Dvořák who was standing by the coat-rack in the corner and silently buttoning his overalls. 'Times are hard, indeed; what with the mobilization. But it's all politics, and I'm not interested in it. I'm against persecution, suffering, poverty and, above all, against war. I've experienced one and I've had enough of it for the rest of my life. I know what people have been through. Marriages disrupted, families ruined, blood — even horses suffered . . . I'm against war, that's my politics. And I say so even though I have that drop of German blood, and my wife is German on her mother's side; you can't blame anybody for his origins. Well, have you recovered a little from your stage fright, Mr. Dvořák?' he nodded into the corner where Mr. Dvořák was still buttoning himself up in silence. 'You smoke less now than you used to. Soon you'll feel at home here and maybe you'll stop smoking altogether. Our Zina,' he smiled, taking his snack out of the briefcase, 'is going to have a birthday soon. I really have no idea what to buy for the child. We've just learned that she's going out with a young man called Míla. We've only seen him on a photograph. He seems to be a nice, decent boy from the best of families. But even if we did know him I couldn't ask him about a present, for he'd tell on me. And so I don't know what to buy for her,' he repeated, glancing at the glass box of flies which he had put in the corner. 'Mr. Dvořák, do you have any idea what would be suitable for a seventeen-year-old girl? You probably know more about it than I do. I expect you know what girls of that age like.'

'I don't really know,' the youth by the coat-rack gave an uncertain smile, and glanced at the glass box in the corner. 'A box of chocolate perhaps?'

'Some dress material,' said Zajíc and glanced at the glass box.

'Damn it,' said Beran, 'why dress material! A ready-made dress. A ready-made dress she can put on at once. Mobilization is not,' he added and glanced at the glass box, 'a matter of politics, this is self-defence! This is a fight!'

'Mobilization is not a matter of politics. It's self-defence. A fight,' Mr. Kopfrkingl told Lakmé in the living-room at home after he had climbed onto the chair to hang the glass box with the flies over the piano. 'Mr. Beran told me so in the cloakroom today. Not long ago I ran into Dr. Bettelheim in front of the house, just as he was getting out of his car and so we stopped for a chat. Violence rewards nobody for long, he told me, it can only last a short time, it can't make history. It's possible to stun people, intimidate them, drive them underground. But for how long, he told me. After all, we live in a civilized world, in Europe, in the twentieth century, and he illustrated it with that picture he's got in his surgery. It depicts a woman's abduction by Count Bethlén which failed. But Jews have always been persecuted, he told me, and I can't somehow put that together with his theory that violence is *short-lived*. Standing on the chair Mr. Kopfrkingl glanced at the glass box of flies he was holding in his hand, and said:

'Our German, Willi, is probably right when he says that you have to fight for happiness, justice and peace. Besides, it's no invention of his own; it's probably generally known. Our Mr. Beran would probably maintain the same thing. Perhaps Willi's also right in saying that only strong, one hundred percent people can fight for, and obtain, happiness. I hardly expect the weak ones to do away with persecution, exploitation or poverty; they can only suffer, poor things.' Mr. Kopfrkingl held the glass box of flies on the wall for a while, and then he said: 'When I think of our poor Mr. Fenek . . . but what's the use?' He gave a sad glance as Lakmé looked up at him on the chair. 'Perhaps he's a morphine addict. Morphinism is a terrible killer, my dear,' he gave a nod, and again held the glass box of flies on the wall for a while. 'It's a much bigger killer than alcohol or cigarettes. Poor Mr. Fenek, how could he, with the long nail on his little finger and the little room he's got back there, put an end to exploitation or fight for peace? He's hardly able to pull himself along. He's not even able to have a decent conversation with the director. Poor Mr. Prachař from the third floor, what would he be able to do? I haven't seen Mrs. Prachař for a long time now; let's hope that boy of his won't take after him. Such things can be handed down from one generation to another. Indeed . . .' Mr. Kopfrkingl glanced at the flies in the glass box. 'Heredity has been proved even by *flies*. There's a young man at our place,' said Mr. Kopfrkingl and held the glass box on the wall for a while. 'A Mr. Dvořák. When he came to us first he was a real chain-smoker, but he's getting over his stage fright a little and smokes less now, thank God. Perhaps he'll stop smoking altogether one day. I hope he will from the bottom of my heart . . . Mr. Strauss,' said Mr. Kopfrkingl after he had climbed down from the chair and checked whether the glass box was hanging straight, 'Mr. Strauss is being successful with the application forms for the crematorium. People who deal in confectionery are gentle, kind and good; they appreciate these things. I'm trying to see how to get more agents for the crematorium. I think commercial travellers in children's toys and cosmetics, possibly in jewels too, would be equally suitable. Well, my dear,' he smiled at Lakmé, cleaning the seat of the chair with a cloth, 'I have to take still greater care of you all, you know; my conscience nags me. Dr. Bettelheim above us has a beautiful painting and a car. Willi does too. Well, I don't envy them, I'm glad they have it,' he said sincerely. 'They're good, decent, hard-working people. We have no car, but, on the other hand, we have this blessed home,' he pointed to the living-room, 'and our love. That's much more. You haven't been sad lately, have you Lakmé?' he asked uncertainly, taking a little pair of pincers with which he had been hammering the nail into the wall. 'Is something hurting you, troubling or worrying you?' And after Lakmé had smiled and put her hand on his shoulder, he gave a nod, stroked her black hair and said:

'Our enchantingly beautiful one's going to have her birthday soon, we must give her something nice. Mr. Zajíc suggested some dress material; Mr. Beran said a ready-made dress so she can wear it at once. There's something in that. I'll have to try and find something. I have to call on Mr. Kádner in Ovocný trh soon, which will give me an opportunity to look round for something nice. I wonder what her Mila is like,' he said with a glance at the little pair of pincers he was still holding in his hand. 'According to the photo he seems to be a nice, decent boy, a student from a good family; I wonder whether he's fond of music.'

On the morning of the fifth day, Mrs. Podzimek told Mr. Kopfrkingl in the corridor of the Temple of Death that they'd lost a worker.

'Mrs. Liška's left,' she said in the corridor near the preparation room. 'She was frightened here. I'm almost frightened myself nowadays.'

'Mrs. Liška's left?' said Mr. Kopfrkingl, surprised, taken aback, 'and just now? I've just heard in the tram that the German army is stationed along the border, and that a conference is taking place in Munich. There may be a war now, and she's left? Well, I'm very sorry to hear that,' he said with a glance at the door of the nearby preparation room. 'Poor thing, that means I won't be able to invite her out anywhere now. She was scarcely more,' he sighed as he glanced at the door of the preparation room, 'than a child. But you, Mrs. Podzimek,' he gave a smile, 'you're not going to leave us, are you? Why, you've been here for fifteen years. Why so suddenly? Didn't you read in today's papers about that woman in Lysá who lost the three thousand? A poor mother of two children, she lost three thousand, and instead of notifying the police of the loss, she jumped into the Elbe,' Mr. Kopfrkingl glanced sadly at the door of the preparation room, and then at Mrs. Podzimek. 'She jumped into the Elbe when the three thousand were at the police station. An honest finder had taken them there. That's dreadful. Two more poor, unfortunate orphans.'

In the cloakroom, stooped over the newspaper, Beran and Zajíc were talking about the German army stationed at the border and the conference taking place in Munich to negotiate over the borderland. Standing in the corner by the coat-rack, Dvořák was rummaging in his briefcase.

'No need to be so angry,' smiled Mr. Kopfrkingl at Beran. 'What are you afraid of? What would they occupy us for? What would they be destroying us for? Why, that would mean violence . . .' he recalled Dr. Bettelheim. 'Violence rewards nobody. It can only last a short time, and it can't make history. We live in a civilized world, in Europe, in the twentieth century.' Then Mr. Kopfrkingl gave a smile recalling Willi. 'Why, the poor Germans,' he smiled, 'they're at rock bottom themselves. They're just getting out of poverty and unemployment as well as they can. The fact that they want to be strong doesn't mean anything. Wherever there's strength there doesn't have to be evil. But that's politics,' he waved his hand airily as they all stared at him. 'I'm not interested in politics. Do you know that Mrs. Liška's left? Mrs. Podzimek just told me. She says she was frightened here . . .' Then Mr. Kopfrkingl took the newspaper, turned over the pages and said:

'Have you read about that woman in Lysá? If that woman in Lysá had pulled herself together a little she wouldn't have drowned herself but gone to the police station and it would have been alright. As it is, she has deprived two poor children of a mother. When is Miss Čársky's turn today . . .?' he smiled at Dvořák who was still rummaging in his briefcase by the coat-rack, and Dvořák said:

'She's seventh.'

'Seventh,' said Mr. Kopfrkingl, 'that's a tragedy. It's the first afternoon funeral, which means she won't wait on the dead-end track for a single minute. She'll go into the furnace straight from the funeral hall. We won't be able to pay homage to her beauty by letting her wait for a single second, poor Miss Čárský. I saw her in the preparation room yesterday; she looks as if she were asleep. There's not a trace of the starvation which follows death. She's got a black silk dress and is holding a lovely rosary in her hand. I know the hall will be full of people when we put her on view. She was just about to get married.'

'Sometimes I think I'd prefer to work in the boiler-room,' said Mr. Dvořák by the coat-rack, rather dejectedly, 'or with Mr. Pelikán in the hall where the catafalques are.'

'You too, Mr. Dvořák, you too?' Mr. Kopfrkingl gave a smile. 'What's the matter? Haven't you recovered from your stage fright? Not long ago I was telling my dear one how you've settled down, that you even smoke less and perhaps you'll stop altogether, and now this. The boiler-room,' said Mr. Kopfrkingl, 'is not for you, Mr. Dvořák, you'd degrade yourself. You'd be better off with Mr. Pelikán at the cata-falques.'

Shortly before two o'clock Mr. Kopfrkingl put aside his book about Tibet, switched on the loudspeaker and began to listen to Miss Čársky's service in the funeral hall. A good speaker was giving the funeral oration. 'Do you hear what he says?' said Mr. Kopfrkingl to Dvořák who was standing beside him. 'There's a good orator in there. He says that all human life is nothing but being-to-death; that we realize it now, *here* in this very place. Some philosopher or other said it, and that is exactly what it is. People realize all sorts of things in this place, Mr. Dvořák. All living creatures are destined to die after a short period of life. We were made from dust, dust we are and to dust we shall return. There is darkness before and after us. Life is only a moment in the midst of the dark infinitude. Take people who lived one hundred or five hundred years ago for example, none of them is alive today. They could say the same thing about those who lived before them, and those who come one hundred, two hundred years later will say it about us. New people are being born all the time, and they die all the time in order to be *eternally* dead. At least, that's how some of us perceive it. It would be a sad fate for thinking, living beings if it were really like that. For millions of years new people would be born all the time in order to be immersed again in the unconscious for ever and ever. Why, if that were the case human life would be almost devoid of meaning.'

'But perhaps,' said Dvořák rather dejectedly – and it was the first time he said something like this – 'but perhaps life does have some sort of meaning. In that people do things for their offspring.'

'Mr. Dvořák,' Mr. Kopfrkingl gave an indulgent smile, and there was more pity and sadness than superiority in his smile. 'But Mr. Dvořák, the offspring will die too. One day, in millions of years for example, our earth will become extinct, and so will all life. What will become of all human work, effort and distress then? What has become of the meaning of life for those beings who lived on some planet millions of years ago? You know, Mr. Dvořák, I am fond of my family and I am doing all I can for them. But this does not constitute the meaning of life by any means. This is merely one task of many, my sacred duty. They're now playing Dvořák's Largo,' Mr. Kopfrkingl pointed to the loudspeaker. 'Can you hear that weeping and lamentation? Oh yes. Only a week ago Miss Čárský was going to the office, writing, doing sums, getting ready for her wedding, and now . . . There it is, she had no family, no children; her life was short. Did her life have no meaning then?' I can't even grant you a single moment's peace on the track, my enchantingly beautiful, heavenly one, Mr. Kopfrkingl thought sorrowfully once again. He also said it aloud to Mr. Dvořák. In seventy-five minutes, you, in your black silk dress, will have turned into a dazzling white skeleton, and even that rosary in your hands will completely disappear. And then your dazzling skeleton alone will disintegrate into ashes and fill the tin cylinder, later the urn . . . 'But the soul will not fill it up,' he said then, 'the soul will liberate itself, tear itself away, fly up into the ether, be reincarnated. It won't stray into the urn. It has not been created to exist in a tin container. Yes, human life is nothing but being-to-death, Mr. Dvořák,' said Mr. Kopfrkingl. 'We must take it into account; besides, it goes for animals too, though they don't know about it. However, the meaning of life is not in the being-to-death. Everyone is fond of life; some are afraid of death, they see death as evil, as the end. Premature death, even if it is not the end, is bad indeed. Premature death is only really beneficent if it spares you great suffering.'

'If,' said Mr. Kopfrkingl a little later as Miss Čársky's ceremony in the hall was drawing to a close, 'if we conquered Nature and got rid of death, it would probably be our misfortune. That's to say, if we got rid of death, there'd be no escape from suffering. Which means that there would have to be no question of there being any suffering before that could happen; and people would have to be angels first as well, because they are the cause of suffering. So we can see that eternal life, without death, is not possible *on this earth*; that eternal life, without death, is possible only when and where there is no suffering, and so is possible only in some kind of paradise. So you can see that eternal hell, as it is taught, is utter nonsense. Eternal hell cannot exist, though on the other hand, eternal heaven or nirvana, as the Tibetans call it, can. Thus death on earth is a blessing. A blessing because there are both people and suffering on earth, and not angels or paradise. If death did not exist, Mr. Dvořák,' said Mr. Kopfrkingl, listening attentively as Miss Čársky's ceremony had finished and Mr. Pelikán was up there opening the curtain, 'if death did not exist, we'd be unable to turn to dust as the Bible says. We could not be reborn of dust, and reincarnation would cease to make any sense . . . Indeed, none of this is necessary in paradise, heaven, nirvana. There would be no funerals and so these ovens of ours would be of no use. The state would not have had to supply them and so even the most humanitarian state in existence could write off its crematoria. Poor Miss Čárský,' said Mr. Kopfrkingl. 'I'm just about to take her to the furnace. To the No. 1 furnace, take a look. And she was on the point of getting married. She will be reborn, but what's the use? Her death is premature and that's bad. Premature death,' repeated Mr. Kopfrkingl, glancing at the thermometer, 'premature death is beneficent only if it spares you great suffering. Well, it seems to me,' he glanced at the thermometer, 'that it's not the case for Miss Čárský.'

As Mr. Kopfrkingl was passing Mr. Fenek's porter's lodge later that afternoon, the eccentric crept out of his den and stopped him to ask if he had the morphine yet.

'I told you that Mr. Reinke is not in Prague,' replied Mr. Kopfrkingl. 'You must be patient. He's got no time to think about morphia. The German army's stationed along the border and a conference is taking place in Munich. There may be a war and you're thinking of morphia, Mr. Fenek.' Mr. Fenek crept back inside. Look at that. Mr. Kopfrkingl was almost taken aback. I show him a little bit of strength and it completely frightens him, poor thing. 'I'm going to the bookbinder's to have a book bound, Mr. Fenek,' he told him, to calm him down a little. 'And also to look round for a dress. My daughter is going to have her birthday . . .' and he stepped out of the building onto the courtyard. At the gate he exchanged greetings with Mr. Vrána, the watchman, who was there on account of his liver, and then went by tram to see Mr. Kádner, the bookbinder, in Ovocný trh.

'Mr. Kádner,' said Mr. Kopfrkingl in the bookbinder's shop to a little old fat man in a stiff white collar with a red bow tie who was standing behind the counter, and took out some papers from his briefcase. 'Mr. Kádner, I'd like to have these pages bound. They're my second favourite reading matter which I've had in my library for years. In my library for years right beside the yellow book about Tibet, which you also bound some time ago. It's the *Cremation Act* . . . ,' he said, 'of 7 December 1921 and the Regulations of 9 October 1923. It's not much, only a few pages, but perhaps they could be bound in some sort of pretty black binding with a silver border and a sprig of cypress. Would there be room for the ornament on the spine too?'

'A narrow border certainly,' said Mr. Kádner in the stiff white collar and the red bow tie, inspecting the thickness of the pages. 'But not the cypress and the title, they will have to go on the cover only. But it will take some time, Mr. Kopfrkingl, a week. There's the mobilization, and we have received orders from the Red Cross. Lucie . . .' An elderly woman in spectacles appeared behind the counter. She wiped her hand, which was apparently wet, on a piece of cloth, gave a bitter smile and Mr. Kádner said:

'Lucie, show Mr. Kopfrkingl some nice mourning samples for the binding.'

Upon leaving Ovocný trh, Mr. Kopfrkingl headed for Rytířská Street, and there he halted in front of the window-display of a ready-made clothes' shop in order to look inside for a dress for Zina. In the window numerous white lace collars were laid out, and there were also several female figures dressed in pretty light-coloured floral dresses. In the corner stood a figure of a pink-faced girl in a black dress; it was a black silk dress. Zina could wear that dress, thought Mr. Kopfrkingl, when she goes out, to the theatre, to meet her Míla, or for walks with us, her parents. That dress is made just for her; she'll come with me tomorrow and try it on. Then Mr. Kopfrkingl noticed the white lace collars and said to himself, what if I bought something for Lakmé as well; although my heavenly one is not celebrating anything just at the moment, she'd certainly be pleased with a white lace collar. It would be just right for her best dark dress . . . and he entered the shop. That collar will look nice on her dark dress, she'll be pleased, he said to himself with satisfaction as he left the shop. What else should I buy for Zina, the sweet good soul? Then he remembered the picture of the wedding procession in Mr. Holý's shop on Nekázanka Street. As I am here I might as well drop in, he thought. That wedding procession would also be a nice present; girls like weddings. It would look nice by the window in the dining-room instead of the one of the Minister of Pensions, which we could hang on the wall over the door. I wonder if Mr. Holý still has the picture . . . and indeed, Mr. Kopfrkingl went to Nekázanka Street and dropped in at Mr. Holý's. Behind the counter stood his beautiful pink-faced daughter in her black dress and she was measuring a frame. 'That wedding procession as a birthday present?' she smiled at Mr. Kopfrkingl, and it was a beautiful, gentle smile. 'Oh yes, it's still here somewhere. Wait a moment, I'll get my father . . .'

'A beautiful wedding, Mr. Kopfrkingl,' said Mr. Holý as he brought the picture out. 'When I remember my wife and our wedding for example, which was a good twenty years ago, it's not true any more. And now she's been *over there* for nine years, poor thing . . .' he pointed somewhere behind him, in the direction of Masaryk Railway Station. 'There's a birch tree by her grave . . . Well, it's a print,' he said looking at the picture. 'I'll charge you only for the frame and glass. Nine crowns. We'll wrap it nicely for you as it's a birthday present. Marta dear,' he said to his pink-faced daughter, 'get that silver paper with the red poppies.'

'Father, what's that? Those flies hanging over the piano,' said Zina that evening when she came home.

'But Zina, my little one, they've been there for a week already,' smiled Mr. Kopfrkingl gently. 'An unfortunate wretch gave them to us. Hadn't you noticed them before? Well, it seems to me, my darkhaired beauty, that you're very much taken up with something,' he gave a smile for it occurred to him that her mind was probably fully occupied with her Míla, whom they'd only seen on the photo.

'You're probably thinking of your Míla, my beauty,' he smiled. 'Well, there's nothing wrong with that. To judge by his picture he seems to be a nice, decent boy, a student from the best of families.' Then he said:

'The flies have been hanging there over the piano for a week already, and they're interesting. One of them is called funebris, the funereal one. That's the one, the big black tufted fly. If it had a coffin and stood beside it, it would look like Mr. Špaček in his uniform. Mr. Špaček is an undertaker. The other flies are called fruit flies, they're being used in the study of genetics. Zina dear,' Mr. Kopfrkingl smiled kindly at Mili, who was standing in the corner with the cat, eating a chocolate ring and staring. 'You're going to have your birthday soon. I'd like to buy you a nice silk dress for going out, the theatre, the cinema, walks with us, and, of course, with your Míla . . . You ought to come with me tomorrow to try it on. I've picked one out on Rytířská Street. I've bought a nice white lace collar in the same shop for our *ethereal one*,' he said. 'It's for her best dark dress. Mili,' he smiled at the cat in the corner, and then went to Mili, who was finishing his chocolate ring, and stroked the cat.

'How very clean our good Rosana is,' he said. 'How she enjoys her food. She has enough milk today.'

VII

The Sudetenland had been occupied and Kopfrkingl's flat was glowing.

'How nice our dear dining-room is,' said Mr. Kopfrkingl to Lakmé by the table in the kitchen putting sandwiches on a big tray. 'Our dear dining-room looks as if a wedding was taking place in it. Our enchantingly beautiful one is sitting at the head of the table . . .' Mr. Kopfrkingl pointed to a kitchen chair. 'Her Míla here, two class-mates of our enchantingly beautiful one, Lenka and Lála here, Jan Bettelheim here and over there Vojta, son of the unfortunate Mr. Prachař from the third floor. You know, my gentle one,' he said to Lakmé, who was now putting salted almonds into little bowls with her delicate fingers. 'When I look at them all sitting in that dear dining-room of ours, they remind me of a scene from some beautiful old picture by a famous painter. It was clever of Zina's Míla to bring his camera along. If the pictures come out well they'll be a beautiful memory for the rest of our lives.' Then Mr. Kopfrkingl said, putting chocolate rings and cakes on the second tray: 'Indeed, our Zina is beautiful, like you, my heavenly one, and your late mother. And how well she looks in that new black silk dress! It's just right for going out, the theatre, walks with her parents . . .' Mr. Kopfrkingl gave a smile. If she had fair hair instead of black like both her dear class-mates, she'd look like an angel. Should the young Míla get her . . . but I hope he will,' he gave a smile. 'He's a very nice boy. His photo didn't lie and he's from a good family. His father, Mr. Janáček, is a great expert on machines, and he's also some sort of official in the Czech Sokol association, and Míla appears to be very happy with Zina. I noticed his glance during the toast. His name Miloslav could be more traditional though, like Svatobor or Zlatko, for example. Miloslav is too mundane, but that doesn't matter. Names don't mean anything, as you say, my dear. Míla is interested in physics, things electric, and machines; besides, I've always been interested in these things myself, I must ask him whether he's fond of music . . .'

'They're still children,' smiled Lakmé, adjusting the white lace collar on her dark dress. 'After all, it's what you call puppy love. Many things can still happen . . .'

'Of course,' said Mr. Kopfrkingl with a glance at the white lace collar, 'many things can still happen. The future is always uncertain. None of us knows what's in store for us, or what we shall escape from, the only certainty we have in our lives is death. But everybody remembers his puppy love with pleasure. Our enchantingly beautiful one will remember it for the rest of her life. Will the two wine bottles be enough . . .?' asked Mr. Kopfrkingl, putting spoons on the table. 'Perhaps they will. I'm abstemious, I've got coffee and you've got your tea in there, my heavenly one. Mili's got a sweet tooth and so has Jan Bettelheim, they'd rather eat chocolate rings and cakes. Did you notice how little they drank during the toasts? They certainly won't become alcoholics, thank God . . . Well, in fact, the bottles are only for the two girls, Misses Lenka and Lála, and Zina, her Míla and the son of the unfortunate Mr. Prachař. That boy Vojta drank a lot, let's hope he won't be like his father, it would be a pity. However, we mustn't suspect the worst, nor about the smoking either. I haven't seen Mrs. Prachař for a long time now but we mustn't let on, Zina especially. I wonder how Míla's going to take pictures of us. God willing, the pictures will come out well. It would be a beautiful memory of this day.'

'I don't think I've told you yet, Roman,' smiled Lakmé, taking plates out of the dresser, 'that Willi has written. Look, I've found his postcard in here,' and she took the postcard out of the dresser. 'I hope it doesn't matter that I forgot. It came this morning. He's inviting you and Mili to see a boxing-match next week. He says that you should see something real for once . . .'

Mr. Kopfrkingl took the card, read it and with a glance at the dresser returned it to Lakmé, smiling.

'Next Wednesday at the Youth Club,' he gave a smile. 'Well, perhaps we could go, what with Willi asking us out and all that. We haven't really talked properly ever since that Sudetenland affair. But why is he asking us to the Youth Club? It's a Czech club, after all, and a boxing-match of all things! I had no idea that he enjoys boxing, or did I?' Then he said: 'Mili will no doubt be surprised when I tell him. He's never seen a boxing-match before, it'll be something of a revelation for him. I hope it won't have a bad influence on him, the good boy; I think that boxing is rather rough. Get Zina, my gentle one . . .'

Lakmé ran out to get Zina. Zina came at once; she had on her new black silk dress and looked very nice in it. They picked up the dishes, almonds, plates and spoons from the table, and went out. In the doorway Zina said:

'I didn't know that we'd be serving sandwiches and sweets now. I thought they would be on the table during the toast.'

'It's better to bring out one thing after another,' Mr. Kopfr-kingl gave a smile. 'If everything was laid out on the table there'd be no surprises. It's just like the casket which contains something new each time you open it. It's better to see things gradually, one after another, rather than all at once . . .'

In the dining-room they were indeed sitting as though in a scene from a beautiful picture. Perhaps it was because they all sat at the table together, the cat having joined them into the bargain. Mili was holding her by the belly over the edge of the table, Jan Bettelheim was pulling her tail and Vojta was holding a glass of wine to her snout. Both Lenka and Lála were laughing. They did indeed have fair hair; Lenka was slim, Lála rather fat. Míla was laughing, turning his head and looking over his shoulder at the camera which was resting by the newspaper on the cabinet behind his back.

'Well, have something to eat, dear children,' urged Mr. Kopfrkingl in a kind manner, when the dishes had been put on the table. 'Everything must be eaten up. Young ladies . . .' he smiled at Lenka and the fattish Lála, 'Mr. Ja-náček, boys . . .' he turned to Jan Bettelheim and Vojta, and then he said: 'Mili, don't torture the innocent one. Let her go. We can call her when we start taking pictures.'

'Oh yes, that's a French minister,' said Mr. Kopfrkingl when Míla glanced at the spot over the door where the Nicaraguan president was now hanging as the picture of the wedding procession had replaced it by the window beside the wall chart. 'A former professor at the Collège des Sciences Sociales, later Minister of Pensions . . . It used to hang by the window beside the wall chart,' he pointed. 'Now there's a picture of a wedding procession hanging there instead. I bought this wedding procession,' Mr. Kopfrkingl got up and took down the picture of the wedding procession, 'for Zina from Mr. Holý on Nekázanka Street. Mr. Holý is a lonely old fellow, a widower; he lost his wife nine years ago. He has a beautiful pink-faced daughter, called Marta. A wedding, dear children,' Mr. Kopfrkingl smiled at the picture he was still holding in his hand, 'is a big event. It happens only once in a lifetime, it can never be repeated; in fact, you take it with you to your grave. Of course, there are people who divorce each other,' Mr. Kopfrkingl shook his head and put the picture back on the wall. 'They divorce each other and remarry, such things happen from time to time . . . But whether this is wise or good,' Mr. Kopfrkingl shook his head, 'that's a question, I don't agree with it. A husband should be faithful to his wife and a woman should be faithful to her husband. A wedding is a sacred ceremony.' Mr. Kopfrkingl glanced at the wedding ring on his finger and seated himself at the table. 'This kind of sacred ceremony should take place only once in your life. It's almost akin to pronouncing somebody dead,' Mr. Kopfrkingl gave a smile, 'the most responsible and sublime official act which can be carried out in this world. Or a funeral, which also takes place only once in your life. Well, Mr. Janáček, so you've brought your camera along,' he glanced at the boy. 'Do you think it will be alright in this light?'

'It will,' replied Míla swiftly. 'Shall I try it now?'

'Perhaps we could wait until you've had something to eat,' said Mr. Kopfrkingl. 'A fellow looks better when he's *full*. He looks kind of more real then, more *alive*. And indeed, you haven't had anything to eat yet,' he pointed to the table. 'Go on and have something to eat, Mr. Janáček, look what we've got here. Young ladies,' he turned to Lenka and the fattish Lála, 'you're not eating either, or perhaps you're slimming . . .' and inwardly he thought: Slimming, that's a good thing. One can at least save on the wood . . . and he said aloud: 'After all, you're still young.' Then he urged Vojta and Jan to have something, and Zina poured the wine. The two fair-haired girls and Vojta took a drink and helped themselves to sandwiches. Jan and Mili took cakes, and then Vojta fixed his eyes on the bookcase.

'That's my little bookcase,' Mr. Kopfrkingl gave a smile. 'It contains books you can read time and time again, and they're still as charming and exciting as they were the first time. You never get tired of them . . . Zina dear,' Mr. Kopfrkingl turned to Zina, 'turn on the radio; there's a nice opera on just now. It'll form a kind of background or complement to our conversation . . .' Then he said:

'That bookcase contains the two books I like best of all. The yellow one,' he pointed into the distance, 'is about Tibet and the Dalai Lama. The second one beside it, bound in black covers, is not really a book; it's only a few pages long. It was almost impossible to have them bound, but they are precious pages. They're *laws* . . . But it occurs to me that we haven't seen the papers yet,' said Mr. Kopfrkingl while the music from the radio struck up. It was a lively Siciliana from Verdi's "Sicilian Vespers", sung by an excellent singer . . . 'We haven't seen the papers yet although we live in such eventful times, particularly after the occupation of the Sudetenland. Great things are happening nowadays,' he said, fetching the newspaper which had been left lying beside Míla's camera on the cabinet. Turning over the pages he read:

'"Boy, a minor, drove car ... A bricklayer who was pushing a hand-cart was knocked down, and a coachman fell from his seat but was only slightly injured. As it was established later, the car was driven by a seventeen-year-old boy, a minor. He took his father's car for a drive around Prague ..." This couldn't happen to you, Mili,' Mr. Kopfrkingl smiled at Mili, who was eating a chocolate ring. 'We don't have a car. You only have that game of yours of dividing cars into coloured, green and white ones ... This is more likely to happen to Jan, they have a car,' Mr. Kopfrkingl smiled at Jan Bettelheim, who appeared to be listening to the music. 'But Jan is a nice, well-behaved boy who prefers music, going to the opera and concerts to taking his uncle's car. Your uncle,' Mr. Kopfrkingl put the newspaper aside for a moment and looked kindly at Jan, 'is a rare person. An excellent physician. An outstanding expert. Besides, it's a wonderful thing to be a doctor. I read once that a physician is a kind of angel among people, he helps those who are stricken. What's more beautiful than helping those who are stricken? A doctor helps relieve people of their pain and suffering ...' he said slowly ... and then after a moment's silence in which the singer finished her Sicilian aria, he said: 'Dr. Bettelheim is also an outstanding expert on pictures ... That was the Siciliana from Verdi's "Sicilian Vespers".' Then he picked up the newspaper again and read:

'"Live aerial killed woman",' he read and glanced at Lakmé, who was just at that moment adjusting the white lace collar on her dark dress. 'How careless women are. They are not the slightest bit careful. If that woman were to be cremated, all that would remain of her in an hour and a quarter would be two kilograms of ashes. Mili ...' he looked up at the boy as the radio began to play the Mignon song about the country where the lemon trees bloom. 'You also

(78)

get all sorts of ideas. Don't ever dream of putting a banger in your mouth. You might pay dearly for jokes like that. The banger would explode in your mouth and you could become a cripple for the rest of your life. You also go straying about a lot, Mili,' Mr. Kopfrkingl shook his head, looking for another piece of news in the paper. 'You ought to stop it. Look at Jan,' he indicated Jan Bettelheim. 'Whenever he goes out, he goes only as far as the bridge. I'm sure he'd never dream of going to some place in Suchdol and spending the night in a haystack, particularly not now,' Mr. Kopfrkingl raised his head. 'The time is not right for romantic wanderings nowadays. You know perfectly well what has happened; they have occupied the Sudetenland, we are virtually living in a military camp. The police probably haven't much sympathy for romantic boys. That's Marta Krásová singing,' Mr. Kopfrkingl pointed to the radio. 'It's the Mignon song about the country where the lemon trees bloom . . .' and then, after a further moment of silence in which, as it seemed, Jan Bettelheim was listening to Mignon, Mr. Kopfrkingl bent over the newspaper and said:

'There's another thing here. "Serious accident in bed. J. Kašpar from Kosmonosy slept in his bed by the table. One evening he put a big kitchen knife on the table. During the night he had a wild dream, and while he was dreaming he took the knife and stabbed himself in the right arm with all his might . . ." He was apparently left-handed,' Mr. Kopfrkingl shook his head. 'Lucky he didn't stab himself in the heart or stomach, poor thing. Just think,' he put the newspaper aside for a moment, '*even dreams can be* fatal. Well, come on, children, go on eating,' he urged everybody again in a kindly fashion. 'We're having a family party and you don't seem to be having anything. My heavenly one . . .' And Lakmé gave a smile urging everybody to eat and drink, and they all ate. Zina, Míla, Vojta, Lenka, the fattish Lála took a drink, and then Míla glanced at the wall chart by the window.

'Mr. Janáček is looking at that dear gentle wall chart of ours,' Mr. Kopfrkingl gave a smile while a singer began to sing Mephistopheles' cavatina from Gounod's "Faust". 'You probably don't know what this wall chart means. Well, Mr. Janáček, it's our kind of timetable of death,' he said, 'you're interested in things electric, machines, physics, Mr. Janáček. They all have a future, the world is about to be taken over by automation. Personally I like various automatic machines and mechanisms, even if I don't talk much about it. Perhaps the automation and mechanics of this timetable of death will be still more refined one day than it is now,' Mr. Kopfrkingl got up and took the chart down from the wall to the accompaniment of Mephistopheles' song on the radio. 'More so than it is now, and then things will get even better and *faster*. It appears to be complicated,' Mr. Kopfrkingl smiled towards the table. 'In reality, however, it's not so complicated. These numbers stand for funeral numbers,' he pointed and the ring on his finger flashed. 'These indicate the length of the services taking place in the hall; these stand for the first and second furnace, and these indicate the length of time it takes for the transformation to occur. This also includes waiting periods on the dead-end track; with two furnaces it can't be otherwise. If there were only one furnace, as is the case in many towns in the country, in Chrudim near Slatiňany for example, the waiting period on the dead-end track would be increased by several hours. When there are two furnaces it increases by thirty minutes at the most. If we had three furnaces the waiting period would be completely eliminated. Then dead-end tracks would not be necessary at all. Everybody would leave the funeral hall straight for . . . Death,' Mr. Kopfrkingl pointed to the wall chart and the ring on his finger flashed anew. 'Death is the only certainty in a man's life. There's nothing certain in a man's life except for the certainty that he's going to die, and so it's necessary to prepare and equip everything which follows after that. That's precisely what cremation does. Cremation is better for one than burial,' said Mr. Kopfrkingl putting the chart back on the wall. 'Precisely because it's more automatic and mechanical, it accelerates the return to dust from which man has come, and, in fact, assists God. But chiefly it helps man himself. Death liberates man from pain and suffering . . .' he looked at Jan Bettelheim, 'removes the wall which surrounds him during his lifetime and restricts his vision. It enlightens him. Don't be afraid of cremation, my dear children,' Mr. Kopfrkingl smiled gently, at which everybody laughed. 'That's Mephistopheles' cavatina from Gounod's "Faust", it's finishing now . . .' he pointed to the radio.

'Has anybody ever come to life after they'd been put into their coffin?' asked Míla, and Lenka, the fattish Lála and Vojta laughed. Only Jan Bettelheim was more serious, he was listening to the radio. A sweet duet for soprano and tenor from the last act of Donizetti's "Don Pasquale" could now be heard . . . and Mr. Kopfrkingl, obviously pleased with the boy's attention, gave a gentle smile and said:

'Of course not, Mr. Janáček, of course not. That has never happened in the course of my profession yet. Not even Mrs. Strunný came to life, although she looked life-like in the coffin, nor Miss Čárský although she was thirty and was about to get married . . .'

'But somebody once did come to life in their coffin,' Vojta objected. 'I read once . . .'

'Me too,' said the fattish Lála . . .

'It has happened once,' Mr. Kopfrkingl interrupted them kindly. 'It has happened but only because that person wasn't really dead. He was really alive when they put him into his coffin but they did not realize it . . . Only two people in history, who were really dead, were given the opportunity to come back to life in the coffin, and they were the daughter of Jairus, and Lazarus. But these were exceptions, a miracle. And then, Jairus' daughter was not in a coffin at all but at home in bed. And Lazarus was not in a coffin either but wrapped in linen, in a tomb cut in the rock. But it is absolutely impossible for anybody to come to life once he has spent an hour and a quarter in the furnace, and his urn has been filled up with ashes,' said Mr. Kopfrkingl sipping his coffee, while the sweet duet from "Pasquale" played on the radio. 'Once the urn is filled up with the ashes it's the end, even if you had a great mind to put yourself together again, jump out and walk about in this wide world of God's for a few days longer like poor Mrs. Strunný or Miss Čárský apparently. Cremation is absolutely reliable and completely rids you of the fear that you might come back to life. The person who opts for cremation will be absolutely certain for the rest of his life that there's nothing to worry about, and that he can die in peace. Even if we believed that cases of people coming back to life can occur nowadays, cremation will spare them all suffering. But my dear children, there really is nothing to worry about,' Mr. Kopfrkingl shook his head with a smile gazing at the table. 'It doesn't happen nowadays. Once somebody is pronounced dead he is perfectly dead. Medical science is reliable nowadays in the diagnosis of death. Dr. Bettelheim would be the best person to confirm it if he were here, and the crematorium is an absolutely reliable mechanism. In the Middle Ages it was possible that people could come back to life now and then. But in those days people didn't even know how to deal with things which were simpler than something like the responsible and sublime act of officially pronouncing somebody dead. They didn't know how to deal with the plague for example. That's the duet,' smiled Mr. Kopfrkingl at Jan, who was still listening rather attentively to the music, 'from Donizetti's "Don Pasquale".'

'But isn't it possible to get the ashes of two different people mixed up . . .?' Jan Bettelheim now asked in a strange manner, for he was apparently not listening only to the radio but also to Mr. Kopfrkingl, and Mr. Kopfrkingl, obviously pleased, shook his head anew.

'Even that can't happen', he said. 'There's no chance of that. It could have happened in the Middle Ages when they used to burn large numbers of heretics at the stake at one and the same time. In the crematorium each person is cremated separately, that is to say, cremated by means of red-hot air. Neither the body nor the coffin must come into contact with flames, that's a rule, there is even a sort of law for that . . . and at each transformation the ashes pass through the grates automatically. However, supposing it could happen,' Mr. Kopfrkingl mused a little, 'supposing it could happen, it wouldn't be such a tragedy as it may seem. That's to say, there's no difference in human ashes. The ashes of a prime minister are the same as those of a waitress; the cremated remains of the director of our crematorium will be the same as those of a beggar . . . It doesn't even matter what sort of blood one has; whether there is or isn't a drop of German blood is absolutely insignificant,' Mr. Kopfrkingl gave a smile. 'All of us have the same forebears, we all come from and return to the same dust, we all have the same origin. And nobody can be blamed for his secondary, transient, actual origin, it has no value whatever. In the end, the same grey-white ashes will remain of everybody.'

The cat then approached the table, and Mr. Kopfrkingl gave a smile and said:

'In some humanitarian countries they even cremate animals after their death. The laws there serve not only people but animals as well. Animals are our brothers and we shouldn't inflict pain even on them. Even the most terrifying beast of prey will not hurt anyone who can understand their sad, reserved souls. Not even a leopard . . .' Mr. Kopfrkingl smiled at Lakmé, who was at that moment sipping her tea, and at her white lace collar which shone prettily

(83)

on her dark dress. 'There's a beautiful passage about it in our beautiful book about Tibet. The passage tells about a boy's face-to-face encounter with a leopard in the jungle. The boy went to sleep in the bush one night, and when he woke in the morning he saw a leopard lying a few feet away from him. They stared at each other and the leopard didn't do him any harm. The boy then became a monk and later the Dalai Lama. This calls for a pure heart; tender, brotherly souls are able to feel it. Go on, my heavenly one,' he stroked the cat 'we'll call you when we start taking pictures. To immortalize your present likeness . . . one day you won't recognize yourself. . .' he added quietly and then he said:

'They're playing a big aria from Bellini's "Norma" on the radio now. It's being sung by a famous Italian singer . . . I think there's still something in the papers we haven't read yet. After the occupation of the Sudetenland we now live as if we were in a camp under siege,' and then, while the Italian soprano was singing the Casta diva from "Norma" on the radio, Mr. Kopfrkingl picked up the newspaper once more.

'Yes, here,' he said. '"Study on girl with two heads". A study about a girl with two heads . . .' he smiled with a glance at the table and read: '"The girls, joined together from birth, had separate heads, necks, upper limbs and chests with the appropriate inner organs, but a joint stomach and only one pair of lower limbs. They had separate spines and therefore a double nervous system, double spinal chord and double brain. Their mental life was quite independent. Each one went to sleep and woke up separately. The monstrosity survived for one year." Just imagine, Jan,' with a smile Mr. Kopfrkingl turned to Jan Bettelheim. 'Supposing this *monstrosity* was cremated, then their ashes were mingled together and nothing happened. It would even have been impossible to separate the ashes in this case . . . Just imagine, Zina, my little one,' he turned to Zina with a smile, 'imagine if you had two heads, you'd be able to do two things at the same time, think of two different things, have two different feelings. That means a double length to one's lifetime. Indeed, what a blessed life. Well, my dear children, let's have one more drink. My heavenly one, give some more to the girls and boys, perhaps not to Jan and Mili, they don't drink, they're still young. They're still playing the aria from "Norma" on the radio.' Then Mr. Kopfrkingl had a sip of his coffee, glanced at the half-empty dishes of sandwiches, chocolate rings and cakes and the bowls of almonds, and said:

'So you've at least had a little something to eat, at least *appeased your appetite* a little . . . Well, Mr. Janáček, how about having a go with the camera?'

They formed a group, Mr. Kopfrkingl taking the cat on his lap and seating himself, with Lakmé, in the middle. Zina and Mili stood next to them, and the other boys and girls positioned themselves behind them. And Míla wagged his finger jokingly, told them to sit still for a moment and took a picture of them to the accompaniment of the divine music from "Norma".

'A photograph,' said Mr. Kopfrkingl after it had been done, 'is, as it were, a kind of eternal conserve of the present, actual time. Pictures are also taken in our crematorium, only you don't have to wag your finger jokingly, nor tell people to sit still for a moment, for the pictures are being taken of people in their coffins. It's not necessary to wag a finger at them, and they're still for ever . . . People buy them for remembrance. The mourners, of course . . .' he added.

Mr. Kopfrkingl kept the cat on his lap and Míla took another picture of him, just with his family – with Lakmé, Zina and Milivoj. This time he did not wag his finger and they sat still for a moment without being told to do so.

'People like remembering a funeral or a wedding when they go through their family albums,' said Mr. Kopfrkingl after it had been done, 'the two most sacred ceremonies in one's life. It's a remembrance for ever.'

Then the son of the unfortunate Mr. Prachař offered to take a picture of them all so that Míla could join them, and Mr. Kopfrkingl gave a nod. Again he sat with the cat on his lap, Lakmé beside him, and the others standing behind them.

'And now you with Zina,' smiled Mr. Kopfrkingl at Míla after this had been done. 'Now I'm going to take a picture of you, if you would care to adjust it for me, Mr. Janáček.' And after Míla had adjusted it and joined Zina, Mr. Kopfrkingl took the picture and said:

'Nothing is certain in human life. The future is always uncertain, and this uncertainty is the source of all fear. But *at least* one single thing is certain in life, and that is death. So in fact, indeed . . . God be thanked for it . . .'

The big aria from "Norma" had finished on the radio and silence set in in the dining-room for a while.

'Perhaps they'll come out well, God willing,' Mr. Kopfrkingl gave a smile, still thinking of the photos. 'It'll be something to remember for the rest of our lives. Put your camera away, Mr. Janáček, in case it gets damaged . . .'

'I would like to ask you a question,' said the fattish Lála with a glance at Míla who was putting his camera into its case, and at Mili who was tucking into almonds, and after Mr. Kopfrkingl had nodded with a kind smile, she said:

'What about embalming? When somebody is embalmed as they used to do in ancient Egypt, for example . . .'

'That would be a longish exposition, Miss Lála,' smiled Mr. Kopfrkingl and made a slight movement with his hand. 'It's actually *against nature*. Against nature because then man does not return to dust whence he came, or because it takes thousands of years before he disintegrates. It is only possible to embalm saints or exceptional figures in history for whom it's no longer a necessity that they return to dust.

They could embalm some pharaohs in Egypt, the Saviour could have been embalmed, Moses too, for example . . . the Dalai Lama could be embalmed in Tibet nowadays . . . but a Mrs. Strunný or a Miss Čárský, that would be a sin. It wouldn't help them, rather the reverse.' Then Mr. Kopfrkingl turned to Zina and said:

'Well, and now, since it's your seventeenth birthday and since you have such distinguished guests, you ought to play something for us on the piano. I'm sure,' he turned to the fattish Lála, 'you're fond of music, Miss Lála, and so is Mr. Janáček . . .' and when they nodded, Mr. Kopfrkingl said: 'Sensitive people love music. That's good. Mr. *Janáček*, are you by any chance related to . . .' but then he turned to Zina again and said: 'Let's enjoy some piano music. Have you got Mahler's "Kindertotenlieder" here, Zina?'

They went into the living-room which contained the piano with the flies hanging above it. Zina began to play some lively music, and Mr. Kopfrkingl remembered that he must tell Mili about going to a boxing-match with Willi next Wednesday.

VIII

In the arena, they sat almost at the ringside. Mili was placed between them like a rose between thorns. Spectators kept trickling in, took their seats and ate choc-ices. Here and there some of them drank beer from bottles or mugs. It was possible to drink beer from bottles or mugs which could then be put under the seats. Both adults and young people were present, and a large number of women as well, more than one would have thought likely. Mr. Kopfrkingl caught a glimpse of an elderly woman in spectacles in the front row. She was at that very moment taking a swig from her beer-mug. He also caught a glimpse of a young pink-faced girl in a black dress with a young man a little distance away. Then he turned slightly to look over his shoulder and noticed a dark woman near the entrance whose profile and breasts reminded him of somebody. Her way of laughing, of twisting her shoulders and her painted lips made him take her for a second-class prostitute. Then he realized that she reminded him of Petite from the Malvaz pub.

'Can you see that lady?' he said to Mili as he slipped his hand into his pocket. 'Not that dark one twisting her shoulders at the entrance, but the one in the passageway who's selling choc-ices. Go on and buy yourself one, and get a programme too.' But Willi forestalled him and gave the boy the money himself. He was the host.

'That dark one at the entrance has a profile and bust which reminds me of someone I know,' he said to Willi after Mili had gone to get his choc-ice and programme. 'The Petite from the Malvaz pub, the second-class prostitute. It may be her. My heavenly one almost forgot to give me your invitation,' said Mr. Kopfrkingl. 'She put it away in the dresser next to the plates.'

'In the dresser next to the plates,' laughed Willi with a glance at the boxing ring, and then he said: 'You should see a manly sport for once. It's good to see a manly sport sometimes. We're not flies in a glass box. We're old soldiers and times are bad. Look how many people are here. Even women . . .' Willi jerked his head.

'Some of them are fond of boxing,' smiled Mr. Kopfrkingl. 'I hope they enjoy themselves. If they like it they should enjoy themselves. It's always better than drinking alcohol or smoking or being a morphine addict . . . I mean drinking alcohol like a confirmed alcoholic. I always thought boxing rather rough,' he twisted his head round with a smile.

'Why rough?' said Willi. 'You could say it's tough. But that's the good thing about it. Times are bad and we need strong men who are one hundred-percent. The weak are not going to bring happiness and justice to people, I've told you that already. Don't you agree? Besides, it's always been so,' said Willi. 'After all, we've already seen it on the front in the War when we were defending German honour. There's often more evil in weakness than in strength.' Then he looked at Mili, who was returning with his choc-ice.

'Have you got the programme?' asked Mr. Kopfrkingl, and after Mili had given a startled cry, he said: 'Well, then, run along and get it so that you'll know who's going to box.' And Mili left them again.

'Sometimes you have to tell Mili everything twice,' smiled Mr. Kopfrkingl glancing towards the entrance where the woman who looked like Petite from the Malvaz pub was still standing. Just at that moment a commotion broke out there. People seemed to surge and jump forward, though no-one could see what was going on. 'There's a commotion at the entrance,' said Mr. Kopfrkingl. 'People seemed to surge and jump forward. So, you said it's tough . . . Surely then, it's not suitable for young people, for that very reason. Combat soldiers or the police should take up boxmg, not these boys. Why, it's a Youth Club!'

'Exactly,' said Willi, 'exactly. Young people must be strong. Even the Czechs understand that. Why, you can see it . . .' he pointed his hand at the overcrowded arena, and then turned to Mili, who had now come back with the programme, and said:

'Well, you've got the programme now, so sit down, it's beginning.'

Mr. Kopfrkingl glanced at the elderly woman in spectacles with her beer in the front row and at the young pink-faced girl in black further off. Then he turned slightly to look over his shoulder. The woman who looked like Petite was still standing at the entrance. The commotion which had started there was slowly coming towards them through the spectators. It could now be seen that it had been caused by two spectators looking for their seats. Then the gong was heard, a spotlight was projected onto the ring and excitement permeated the auditorium.

'Now, pay attention, Mili, and don't be afraid,' said Willi to Mili, who was still licking his choc-ice, no doubt trying to make it last, and holding the programme in his other hand. 'It's not good to be afraid. Fear is mankind's greatest enemy. Well, that's what I maintain . . .' he smiled into the face of his friend Kopfrkingl . . . when everybody turned round a little. The two spectators who had caused the commotion found the seats which they had been looking for, right in front of Willi. Then two juniors climbed into the ring.

'Boxing is a combative sport, ein Kampfsport,' said Willi quietly in German so as not to be heard too easily. 'Kampf Mann gegen Mann. Boxing is not only for the strong and for those who can already do everything, but also for the very boys who lack confidence and courage. In a fight of man against man we learn to use our strength and to fend off the enemy's attacks calmly and safely. Attack and defence are the most important aims in boxing. Let me have a look . . .' he glanced at the programme Mili was holding in his hand. Then he indicated two names which were marked as number one and said: 'That's them, the two in there. This one is from Unity and this one's from AC Prague, an apprentice.'

Then the ropes enclosing the boxing ring vibrated, vibrated like a cobweb: a fat little referee in a stiff white collar and a red bow tie was climbing through and caught the toe of his shoe in them. The crowd roared with laughter. Mr. Kopfrkingl then became aware of the two people who had come in at the last minute and who were sitting in front of Willi. They were a man and a woman.

'Let's hope he doesn't break his leg,' said the woman.

The referee extricated himself from the ropes and straightened his stiff collar and bow tie. He advanced to the centre of the ring, and with an energetic movement of his hand, summoned the contestants. He looked like a furious dwarf.

'Will there be bloodshed?' asked Mili in horror.

'Could be,' Willi shrugged his shoulders. 'It's a combative sport. There's bloodshed in a battle and in war as well. But there shouldn't be any in a boxing-match. Brutal blows are forbidden, in our country at least. Boys in the Hitler Youth, who are being taught how to box in primary school, are trained to give direct hits only; the hook is forbidden . . . der Haken darf im Übungsbetrieb des Jungvolks nicht angewandt werden . . . perhaps it's different in the Czech Youth Club in Prague.'

'Let's hope his teeth don't get knocked out,' said the woman in front of Willi after the referee had waved his arms sending the two contestants to their corners, and Mr. Kopfrkingl took a closer look at her. She held the programme in her hand, and had on her head a hat *with a feather* and a string of beads around her neck. The man beside her was smallish and fat; he was holding a bowler hat on his knees and a stick between his legs.

And then it began, and Mili watched, mouth agape.

'Why, it's nothing,' said Willi after a while. 'There hasn't been a proper punch yet.'

Then there were a few blows, the gong could be heard, and it ended in a draw. Enraged, the fat referee in his collar and bow tie raised his hands and stamped his feet.

'He's dancing a clog-dance,' said the woman with the feather. 'Why isn't he accompanied by a double-bass?'

'Why should he be accompanied by a double-bass?' growled her fat neighbour and gave her a push. 'You're not in a dance-hall. This is a boxing-match!'

The gong could be heard and another couple entered the ring.

'This one is from Unity,' Willi pointed to the programme, which Mili was holding in his hand, 'the blue one is an apprentice from AC Prague.'

The referee stamped his foot and waved his hand. The two started fighting. Now it was livelier, more blows were landed, and Mili watched, mouth even more agape.

'You've got to learn how to do it,' said Willi to Mili. 'You can't do it without instruction. You've got to learn the correct punches, and, what's more important, how to cover and defend yourself. You can't box without proper training. I don't know how things are in this Youth Club, but every boy in the Hitler Youth starts off with individual training. Jeder neue Bewegungsablauf,' he said quietly in German so as not to be heard too much, 'muss zuerst ohne Partner in der Gemeinschaft geübt werden . . .' At that moment the couple in the ring seemed to clinch. The fat referee barged into them and broke them up.

'Let's hope they don't thump him,' said the woman with the feather.

'Why should they thump him,' growled the fat man beside her and gave her a push. 'You're not in a cinema, this is a boxing-match. Yes, a boxing-match,' he bellowed at her. 'You don't thump people here. You box here!'

Then the fight in the ring grew fiercer. The juniors showered each other with blows. The referee hopped around them. The crowd roared and whistled. In the front row, the elderly woman in spectacles took a swig from her beer-mug. The pink-faced girl in black turned away to face the young man sitting beside her. Then the referee began to separate the two contestants.

'Fancy him not having any gloves,' said the woman with the feather.

'He's the referee,' snapped the fat man, giving her a push. 'He's not boxing. It's the two in shorts you should watch.'

Then the one in blue chased his opponent into a corner. The gong could be heard and it was all over. The referee bore down on the one in blue, raised his hand and the crowd broke into an uproar.

'The blue one has won,' said Willi. 'He defended himself well. Die richtige Deckung und Abwehr der Stösse sind grosse Aufgaben. If you knew how to defend yourself like that,' he said to Mili, 'you'd never be in danger. If someone went for you you'd easily hold your own . . .'

The referee leaned over the ropes and gestured vaguely in the direction of the entrance, probably to the next contestants.

'Let's hope he doesn't fall over,' said the woman with the feather.

'What are you worried about,' the fat one snapped at her in a rather brusque manner now. 'Why should he fall over? He's beckoning the next contestants, he's the referee. Be quiet. Shut up,' he hissed.

The third couple entered the ring.

'That's them,' Willi pointed to the programme. 'The one in black is from Unity, the other in red is a butcher's apprentice . . .'

'Why, there's a butcher here,' squealed the woman with the feather pointing to the programme she held in her hand, 'the one in red. There's going to be bloodshed.'

'Don't be daft,' the fat man gave her a push. 'Why should blood be shed? You're not in a slaughter-house. This is a boxing-match. Be quiet for once and watch, or else . . .'

The gong could be heard. The referee stamped his foot and the third fight began. It was fierce right from the start, and Mili was beside himself.

'Don't be afraid,' laughed Willi. 'See, that's a direct hit, der gerade Stoss,' he said quietly in German. 'It's the one from Unity. If you knew how to do it you'd beat everybody.' Then the boxer from Unity dealt the butcher's apprentice another blow, and the apprentice slumped onto the ropes. 'That was the hook, der Haken,' said Willi. The crowd roared and whistled; in the front row, the elderly woman in spectacles took a swig from her beer-mug; the pink-faced girl in black averted her face; the fat referee was furiously stamping his feet and throwing his arms about which made his bow tie jump up and down on his neck. The fat man pushed the woman with the feather and hissed:

'Don't be silly. What're you doing? Watch it.'

'Fancy that, the one with the bow tie is not defending himself,' she squealed turning to her neighbours in excitement. 'Let's hope he doesn't have a stroke. He's some sort of *collector*. Fancy him not having *a green net* . . .'

'Stop jabbering,' growled the fat man, now furious, and banged the stick he had between his thighs on the ground. 'What collector, what green net? I tell you he's the referee, he's not boxing.'

And then turmoil broke out in the ring. Everything seemed to be in a whirl, the contestants showered each other with blows; some hovered in the air, ready to land . . . The fat referee in his stiff white collar and red bow tie was dashing around, jumping, stamping his feet, throwing his arms about and suddenly . . .

. . . suddenly the boxer from Unity crouched, flexed his muscles, his calves and charged . . . and before one could say Jack Robinson the referee flew a metre in the air, *like a butterfly*, waved his hands and fell full length on the floor . . . The boxer from Unity immediately charged again and the butcher's apprentice slumped onto the floor as well . . . Half the crowd roared with laughter, the women leapt up from their chairs, the elderly woman in spectacles threw her beer-mug into the air; the other half resounded with yells, whistles, shouts . . .

'He's dead,' shouted Mili in the midst of the terrible uproar, shaking like a leaf.

'What of it?' Willi gave a smile, 'Was dann . . .'

Standing and pointing at the referee in the ring, the woman with the feather shouted at the fat man: 'What were you jabbering on about him not boxing! It's you who were jabbering on about him being the referee. See, he flew up in the air and now he is lying on the floor! It's you who were jabbering on about it being a boxing-match and that there wouldn't be any bloodshed, that it's not a slaughter-house. See, there is blood . . .' she shouted, pounding him on the back. 'He was jabbering on about us going to a boxing-match. Somebody's speaking German here . . .' Livid with rage, the fat man shook her by the shoulders so much that the feather in her hat and the beads around her neck quivered. 'That was a mistake,' he shouted. 'He was in the way, you idiot. Sit down and shut up. Who'd speak German here? You're not in the Reich, you idiot, you're in Prague . . .' He was pulling at her skirt.

'Nothing to worry about,' laughed Willi, 'he got in the way. Boxing is beautiful, ein schöner Kampfsport,' he said in German. 'It hardens both body and spirit. It develops perceptions, swift reactions, fearlessness and courage. It is the Führer's favourite sport . . .'

In the meantime the referee got up and hopped about; he behaved as if nothing had happened but he was in a towering rage, biting his hand and stamping his feet. The butcher's apprentice got up as well but immediately fell down again. The crowd jumped onto their chairs. Some of them rushed to the ropes; the woman with the feather hit the fat man on the back and shouted: 'He's jabbering on about us being in Prague.' Then she rushed out of the row. The fat man with the hat and the stick jumped up and rushed out after her, thumping her on the back. She screamed and the crowd laughed, shouting: 'Go to it,' and the fat man shouted at them: 'She's a fool. It's the first time she's been to a boxing-match. I'm not going to take her out anywhere. She does it to me all the time. She'll be sent to a lunatic asylum.'

There was noise and confusion at the entrance. The elderly woman in spectacles was there with her empty beer-mug and wet hands, as were the young pink-faced girl in black and the young man. The woman who looked like Petite from the Malvaz pub was also there, twisting her shoulders, laughing and shaking a broken string of beads high up in the air. Mr. Kopfrkingl smiled at her from the crush, and she grimaced at him. Further off, a man was forcing application forms or leaflets on people, but Mr. Kopfrkingl did not manage to get to him, though Willi did, and took an application form or leaflet. Then, at last, they forced their way out onto the darkening street. Under a street lamp, surrounded by several smartly turned-out youths, stood the fat man, his stick leaning against a wall. He was wiping the inside of his bowler hat with a handkerchief.

'Come on, come on,' said Mr. Kopfrkingl to Mili, who was staring at him agitatedly, wanting to say something. 'His wife has run away, probably the shock. The doctor will cure her, come on . . .' Then they walked down the gently sloping darkening street. . .

'So you've seen a manly sport,' smiled Willi at his friend Kopfrkingl and at Mili, who was walking behind them down the gently sloping street. Then, with a glance at the application form or leaflet he had taken at the entrance, he turned to Mili again and said:

'Look, Mili, this is some sort of leaflet or application form. There's something about the training available in the Youth Club. Come and see us, it says . . . Here you are . . . What?' he asked when Mili took the leaflet and said something . . . 'That butcher's apprentice? The one who lost? Is he employed there? . . . Oh no, not at all. He's a butcher's apprentice. He only boxes in the club. Look, you can read about it in the leaflet . . .' Then they turned into another street, well lit by street lamps, and Willi said:

'So you've seen a manly sport and golden Czech youth. I hope you liked it. It's good to see something like this from time to time. We're not flies. Well, what did you think of the Sudetenland?' He smiled at his friend Kopfrkingl. 'You know, we haven't really talked since the Sudetenland. It was a job,' he said, 'but a successful one. The Sudetenland can now breathe freely again,' he lowered his voice slightly for they were passing some people just at that moment. 'German right and justice have won because they were borne along by a pure, strong spirit. Hitler can never fail. If our future is in his hands it's a guarantee of success.'

'Nothing is certain in life,' Mr. Kopfrkingl shook his head with a smile. 'The future is always uncertain. The only certain fact in life is death.'

'Don't worry,' said Willi, still kindly, and with a smile. 'Hitler must be successful because he's fighting for sublime aims. To save a hundred million people from poverty and hunger and for a just order where they will feel as if they were in paradise. There will be no more wrongs, no fear, no suffering . . .'

'That is only possible after death.' Mr. Kopkfringl gave a smile, waving his hand lightly. 'Only after death, in eternal life. When man is no longer reincarnated but reaches his goal, No longer reincarnated, only a pharoah, a saint, or the Dalai Lama reach their goals . . .' Mr. Kopfrkingl gave a smile. 'It's not possible on this earth, in this reincarnation. In this life we can only limit suffering, *shorten* it, nothing more. Dust we are and to dust we shall return,' he smiled at a woman they were just passing. 'Did you notice that young pink-faced girl who was there . . .'

'It's precisely eternal life which is at stake,' Willi interrupted him, more forcibly now. 'The eternal life of our nation. The eternal German Reich, destined to deliver mankind and establish a new and happy order. Today we decide upon Europe's happy future, and I can't think of anyone who wouldn't care about that. Certainly not German fathers and mothers,' he turned round to look at Mili, who was walking slowly behind them with the leaflet in his hand.

'Mili,' Mr. Kopfrkingl turned round as well, and then said with a smile:

'Do we decide Europe's happy future?'

'Of course,' said Willi, a little irritated now, 'not you, of course. You don't feel that drop of German blood of yours. It means nothing to you. *We* fight,' he said harshly. '*You* cowards, don't. Fear makes a man forget his duties ... Well, yes,' he said forcibly when Mr. Kopfrkingl tried to object, 'his *other* duties, the most important duties. He forgets other people, the nation, mankind ... It's easy to give some woman a twenty-heller coin every Friday or Saturday before a cremation. Anyone can give a filthy beggar something now and again, even whores can do that,' he said and turned round a little to look at Mili. 'But to fight for happiness and justice for a hundred million people. *That!* To eliminate unemployment, poverty and national dishonour brought upon it by the enemy. To cleanse it of parasites and insects, to fight for its living space, that is something else, Karl.'

'Living space,' Mr. Kopfrkingl gave a smile. 'Wilhelm, I'll tell you something. I know a thing or two. How coffins are made, for example. When you close the lid of a coffin its cross-section forms a sort of hexagon. This shape gives you as much room as possible. It should be high enough so that the lid doesn't rest on your face and chest. The higher the coffin, the more comfortable it is. The best coffins are those which are capable of taking two. The only space which is of any value,' Mr. Kopfrkingl gave a smile, 'is the one in the coffin. And also the ether, the infinite into which the soul flies up,' he gave a smile.

They arrived at a crossroads with cars and trams passing by. Willi turned round and called to Mili, who was still walking behind them with the leaflet in his hand.

'It may create hell,' said Mr. Kopfrkingl, for it seemed to him that Willi was ominously quiet, 'hell. Hitler may cause it ...'

'Because he fights for happiness and justice for a hundred million people?' said Willi sharply. 'For the eternal life of our nation? For a better, happier Europe? Of course,' he gave a nod, 'it will create hell. For those who deny us life, for those who are taking it from us, for our enemies. Not for decent, honest people.'

At the crossroads, trams and cars were passing by, but only coloured cars – not a single green one among them, not a single military car or prison van, nor a single white one, an ambulance, for angels.

'You probably won't be able to sleep tonight,' Willi said to Mili glancing at the leaflet in his hand, 'because of that boxing-match. No wonder, it's the first you've seen. If you had seen it a couple of times before you'd be used to it, like those apprentices. So now,' he indicated with his head, 'you're home.'

They were in front of the apartment house where the nameplate bearing the name of Dr. Jan Bettelheim, M.D., consultant in skin and venereal diseases, hung beside the door. A number of coloured cars, one of which belonged to Dr. Bettelheim, were parked at the edge of the pavement. 'Where's your car tonight?' Mr. Kopfrkingl asked Willi. 'Erna has got it,' said Willi. 'I'm going home by taxi.'

IX

'Oh, what a Christmas this year,' Mr. Kopfrkingl smiled at Lakmé in the dining-room. She was at that very moment wiping the chair-seats. Then he glanced at the corner with its big Christmas tree, and said: 'What a blessed Christmas. New subscribers for cremation are simply pouring in. Everyone is abandoning the ground in favour of furnaces and ashes. In fact, I've bought the presents for both our *shining ones*,' he said, probably thinking of the children, 'out of the commission. Mr. Strauss is highly successful.

What a good, conscientious fellow. I wonder where he'll be this evening. He had to leave the porter's lodge,' Mr. Kopfrkingl glanced at the spot over the cabinet where the family photograph taken on Zina's birthday was hanging. 'His wife died of consumption of the throat, his son of scarlet fever . . . and I've found another one. Who is it?' he smiled at Lakmé's question as she continued to clean the chair-seats. 'Another good fellow, also conscientious and honest, a Mr. Rubinstein. This time there can't be much doubt that he's Jewish,' he gave a smile. 'Rubinsteins are Jewish. He used to be Liba's salesman, the bed-linen firm, but Liba collapsed. It seems that people somehow buy less bed-linen. Mr. Rubinstein has been selling bed-linen, and now he'll be offering cremation,' he gave a smile. 'It's the same thing really. Both are concerned with making beds and going to bed. One is temporary, in bed for one night, the other is for ever, in the coffin for eternity. Mr. Rubinstein is also fond of music, particularly Mozart and Friml . . . But there's one thing I don't like about Mr. Rubinstein, namely, that he's divorced,' he approached Lakmé standing by the chair and gently stroked her hair. 'I'd rather he wasn't. Or if it has to be, then I'd rather he were a widower like Mr. Strauss or Mr. Holý,' he stroked Lakmé anew. 'However, it's no concern of ours, and it's not for us to weigh and judge; who knows what was behind it. Not every marriage, my heavenly one,' he gave a sigh, 'can be as beautiful and happy as ours. Pity,' he said, approaching the tree in the corner, 'what a pity that your late mother won't come here any more. When I am lighting the candles tonight she will only be able to come as a spirit. On the other hand, Willi is going to *appear* here at five o'clock . . .'

'You talk as if he were a ghost,' smiled Lakmé with a glance at the chair. 'Is Erna coming too?'

'Erna's not coming,' said Mr. Kopfrkingl. 'She probably has her hands full this evening. I expect they're having guests, the Germans from the Prague SdP. Never mind,' he gave a smile, 'Willi's not going to stay long. He just wants to tell me something. Probably that I'm a renegade and a coward,' he gave a smile, 'that I don't have any feelings for my blood, that I'm not performing my duties. Still, he won't say such things on Christmas Eve, I hope,' he smiled anew. 'He's probably coming to wish me a happy Christmas. Well, let him come,' he said then, 'we've got cakes and almonds as well . . . The divine ones are here,' he said quickly, for the sound of the key turning in the lock could be heard.

In the hall, under the Maryborough picture, Zina and Mili were taking off their shoes. On the floor, beside the shelves for shoes, stood a shopping bag which moved slightly by itself.

'They had very big ones there,' Mili exclaimed, all aflame, 'like this. Such huge ones. But she bought two smaller ones,' he pointed at Zina.

'Anežka also bought two smaller ones,' said Zina. 'Two smaller ones are better than one big one, silly.'

'Well hurry up, my dears, go and fill the bath,' urged Mr. Kopfrkingl kindly, gazing at the bag which moved by itself beside the shelves for shoes. 'I know they're opening their gills and gasping for breath. Anežka is going to kill them towards evening.'

They ran into the bathroom. Mr. Kopfrkingl took the carp out of the bag, put them carefully on the bottom of the beautiful white bath and turned the taps on. Then he stood over the bath with bowed head as if standing over a catafalque, Zina and Mili beside him. They watched the carp tossing about on the bottom, and the water filling the bath little by little. They watched the carp as they grew more lively and then, when there was enough water, as they began to swim calmly around.

'Sweet,' Mr. Kopfrkingl raised his head and glanced at the ventilator from which a cord was hanging, fastened on a hook under which there was the yellow butterfly on the wall. 'Nothing is going to happen to the little carp now. The little carp are in their element now. Let's leave our dear bathroom.'

'Why is Anežka going to kill them for us?' asked Mili, also glancing at the ventilator. 'Can't you do it?'

'Why, my child,' smiled Mr. Kopfrkingl kindly. 'Of course I can do it. It's only that I don't like doing it. Anežka is an old hand, she's been doing it for us for years. Don't you know why? Why, because it gives us a pretext to give her something for Christmas,' he gave a smile and added: 'She's a good old soul.'

Towards evening Anežka came to kill the carp.

Mr. Kopfrkingl heard her talking to Lakmé in the hall. He came out into the hall, greeted the good old soul kindly and called towards the kitchen:

'My gentle ones, come into the dining-room, Anežka is here.'

And inwardly he thought, I say it as if I were announcing an executioner.

'Don't go into the kitchen yet,' he said to Zina and Mili as he stood by the tree in the corner of the dining-room. 'Stay here for a while. You don't have to see it. This is no,' he smiled at Mili, 'boxing-match. Where's Rosana?' he asked and Mili said: 'In the kitchen.'

Mr. Kopfrkingl approached the cabinet, gazing at the family photograph for a while. He sat there in the middle, next to Lakmé, with the cat on his lap, with Zina and Mili standing on either side of them. Then he gazed for a while at the standard lamp, which was turned off, and at the chair beneath it. Then he reached for the newspaper on the cabinet.

'"A nine-year-old boy is missing"', he read after he had turned to the inside pages. '"He left home three days before Christmas Eve, and has not come back so far. His parents and the police have been looking in vain for . . ."' Mili turned away towards the window, and Mr. Kopfrkingl had to smile. Then the click of the kitchen door could be heard, and Mr. Kopfrkingl turned round.

'The carp are in the kitchen now,' he nodded at the children. 'There's room on the table now, and Anežka is getting the board, knife and mallet out . . . ' Then the sound of a blow could be heard from the kitchen.

'One of them is now dead,' Mr. Kopfrkingl gave a nod, glancing at the wall chart by the window, that most sublime timetable. 'Which one could it have been? The smaller or the bigger one? The wall surrounding him has collapsed and he has seen the light. His soul,' he straightened the newspaper, which he was holding in his hand and walked slowly with it towards the bookcase, 'is now in the ether.' Then he looked at the newspaper again and read:

'"A woman allegedly committed suicide because of hunger. This morning at 8 o'clock, in Dr. S.' villa, the police found . . ." ,' Mr. Kopfrkingl read the news item to the end and glanced at Zina, who was at that very moment arranging her hair in front of the small mirror. Then the sound of a second blow could be heard from the kitchen and Mr. Kopfrkingl, standing by the bookcase, nodded his head.

'Now the second one is dead,' he said, glancing at the wall chart by the window, the most sublime timetable. 'Which one could it have been? His wall has collapsed too, and his soul is in the ether. You'll be taking their air-bladders,' he smiled at Mili and took the book about Tibet out of the bookcase. 'You'll play with them as you have always done ever since you were small. But they're not really the souls of the carp, that's only what people call them. They're air-bladders. Their real souls could have been reincarnated by now,' Mr. Kopfrkingl opened the book, 'possibly into cats. They're our younger brothers. We shouldn't really kill and eat them, it's cruel. Well, there you are. In a moment your heavenly mother will put them on the kitchen stove, on that little furnace of ours, and fry them,' he said, putting back his book about Tibet and taking out the copy of the laws on cremation bound in black covers. 'They'll arrive on our festive dining-table at seven o'clock. But God has arranged it so and that's good. By eating them on Christmas Eve we *accelerate* their rebirth. The Saviour ate them too,' said Mr. Kopfrkingl, putting back the copy of the laws on cremation. 'He also ate lamb . . .' Then he gave a smile, put away the newspaper in the cabinet and extended his hands to Zina and Mili.

'Come, my gentle ones,' he said, 'we'll give Anežka her present. A pretty red apron.'

When Anežka had left, Willi came.

He exchanged greetings with Lakmé and the children in the hall and took off his coat. He had on an elegant new suit. Then he entered the dining-room. There was a bottle of wine ready on the table.

'You've got a nice tree there,' said Willi. 'What about the carp, have you got that?'

'Two,' Mr. Kopfrkingl gave a smile. 'My heavenly one is going to fry them in a moment. In a moment she's going to put them on that little furnace of ours. Her late mother,' he said, 'used not to fry the carp. She used to make *sweet-jellied* carp, in a *foreign style*. We do them in the Czech style. You've come to tell me that I'm a renegade and a coward . . .' Mr. Kopfrkingl gave a smile.

'I never said that,' Willi turned away from the tree. 'I only said that you don't feel your German blood, and that *we* fight for happiness and justice. We,' he gave a laugh, seating himself at the table, 'strong people who are one hundred-percent. I said,' he said and poured a little wine into his glass, 'that fighting for sublime goals doesn't create hell for decent people, but for our adversaries. For war-mongers. Do you like violence?' Willi smiled in a kind of attentive manner, if it is at all possible to smile in an attentive manner, and raised the glass to his lips. When Mr. Kopfrkingl did not answer immediately, he said: 'Do you like those who are responsible for our poverty? Do you keep your fingers crossed on their behalf? So that they can bury us still deeper? For them to make beggars of us? Have you ever seen a *bloodletting*?' he asked lightly and said: 'They cut the vein here, on the arm, and put leeches on it. They used to do it in the Middle Ages to fight the plague . . . I always thought,' he said and took another sip of wine, 'that you were against violence, that you're concerned with peace, justice and everybody's happiness. Well, look here,' he said and rapped the table with his fingers, 'to give you some proper information for once. I always thought that you didn't like war, that you haven't forgotten how people suffer in war, and not only people. You talked about horses once . . . Well, this republic is an enormous barrel of gunpowder. The source of a new World War. Our enemies' bastion.'

'It's a humanitarian state,' objected Mr. Kopfrkingl. 'A humanitarian state, it has good laws . . .'

'Laws on cremation,' Willi interrupted him. 'We've got them, too. Every humanitarian state has them, except perhaps for the Vatican which doesn't recognize cremation. But why didn't this humanitarian state grant us, us Germans, the right to self-determination? Why did it make it difficult for the Germans in the Sudetenland to send their children to German schools? Why did they make raids on our people in the borderland and shoot them? What . . .?' he said in answer to Mr. Kopfrkingl's objection as to whether it was true. 'Is it true? Don't you know? And what about the poverty here? You yourself have admitted to that, that you haven't been able to put an end to poverty entirely. There are beggars here, there are women here who sell skinned cats in the markets instead of rabbits . . . That would not be possible in the Reich even now, although we're not yet home and dry by a long chalk. I'd stake my life on it that there's not a single beggar in the Sudetenland today, and how long is it since the Führer liberated them?' he said and took a swig. 'No, Karl, to make things clear. It must not come to war. Violence must be suppressed, everywhere. This republic is lost. Poland will not lift a finger for it. Beck made an agreement with Goering on the share which will fall to him once the republic is liquidated, and the Little Entente has fallen into decay. It's over.'

'Has it really gone that far?' Mr. Kopfrkingl shook his head and wanted to add something, but Willi interrupted him forcefully.

'Even further,' he said. 'This republic is only *one* bastion of the enemy. There are still other enemies and the Führer is going to settle accounts with them too. We Germans,' he said and gave a smile, 'are destined to bring order. We are going to establish a new, happier, and just order in Europe,' Willi rose, crossed the dining-room and then halted by the cabinet.

'We're upholders of a strong, proud spirit,' he said, glancing at the family photograph in which Mr. Kopfrkingl sat in the middle, with the cat. 'Pure Germanic blood flows in our veins. Blood is our greatest honour and it cannot be outweighed either by education or by gold . . . it's a gift from above . . . Yes,' Willi glanced at his friend Kopfrkingl, 'no-one who's got it will disclaim it.

'We're upholders of a luminous civilization,' he went on, gazing at the picture of the wedding procession and at the wall chart by the window, the most sublime timetable, the timetable of death. 'We know what life is. We understand it as no other nation does, we got it from above as a christening present. You too . . .,' he turned to his friend Kopfrkingl, 'especially you. But why! Because you have German blood which you won't disclaim. Do you think it's a coincidence?'

Willi smiled at the picture of the wedding procession. 'This is no coincidence. This is predestination.'

'We are going to establish a superior, universal morality, and,' he approached the Christmas tree on which there were many candles waiting to be lit, 'a new world order. You're one of us. You're an honourable man, sensitive, a man of responsibility, and most of all . . .' Willi turned round, 'strong and brave. A pure Germanic soul. Nobody can take it from you, mein lieber Karl. You can't take it away, even if you wanted to a hundred times over, *not even you yourself*. Because it's been given to you from above. It's your gift too. Your *predestination*. You're one of the chosen,' Willi pointed to the ceiling as if pointing to the sky. Mr. Kopfrkingl was sitting behind the table, on which stood a bottle of wine and a half-empty glass, and gazed at Willi, who was standing in front of the Christmas tree, smiling softly. There was a moment of silence and then a rap on the door could be heard. Lakmé came in carrying a bowl of almonds.

'Willi will *not have* almonds today,' said Mr. Kopfrkingl. 'Thank you, my noble one. We'll join you soon.'

When Lakmé left, Willi seated himself at the table and, as it seemed, emptied his glass with relish. Mr. Kopfrkingl refilled it.

'I must be going,' said Willi kindly. 'Erna's waiting. We're spending Christmas Eve in the Casino. In the German Casino on Růžová Street,' he moved his hand, 'with that white marble entrance and the three steps. There's going to be a big gathering. Factory owners, deputies, professors from the German Charles University. Only some of them of course . . . I'm going to confer about something with Boehrmann, the leader of the Prague SdP. You won't,' he said, 'find a more luxurious establishment in Prague than our German Casino, Karl. The way we've furnished it,' he looked round the walls of the dining-room, 'is simply a miracle. Beginning with the carpets, mirrors and pictures, and ending with the lavatories and bathrooms. Beginning with the food and ending with the service. There are *excellent waitresses, barmaids and hostesses.* Magnificent, ravishing women, they're breathtaking,' he gave a smile. 'They're German of course. Only fellow-countrymen are admitted to the Casino. German nationality. No Czechs. We won't put up with trouble-makers and spies in our own house. Well, I'm going to Vienna and Berlin in January,' Willi rose. 'I'll be given a new car in Berlin. Karl,' he extended his hand to his friend Kopfrkingl, who had risen as well. 'Everything depends on one's ability to see the whole. To think about the future. About a better life for our children. About a more joyous life for mankind. Well, it seems to me that you're better informed about Tibet than about happenings here at home.' He gave a smile. 'Well, merry Christmas and all the best for the New Year. You've got a loose curtain there,' he nodded his head in the direction of the window. Indeed, the outer edge of the curtain had slipped off its cord and was hanging loose below the rod. 'Well, have a good time. I'll just say goodbye to the family,' he said.

By seven o'clock Lakmé and Zina had laid the dining-table. Both had their best dresses on. Zina wore the black silk dress she had received for her birthday; Lakmé had the dark silk dress with the white lace collar. Mr. Kopfrkingl lit the candles on the tree and turned on the radio. Then they all seated themselves at the table.

'I thought,' said Zina, 'that we'd light the candles when we start giving presents.'

'It's better to light them before dinner,' smiled Mr. Kopfrkingl. 'After all, they're not lit often, only once a year. They're lit more often on graves and catafalques. Well, Christmas is really beginning now,' he pointed to the radio on which carols could be heard, 'and we have to remember all these dear good souls of ours who are not with us or who don't understand us. Our enchantingly beautiful one,' he smiled into the corner where the cat was licking her plate, 'our eternal Rosana. Our aunt from Slatiňany, that faithful good soul of ours, always ready to help, who, had she been a Catholic, would certainly be canonized when she dies, and who is a saint even during her lifetime. Our gentle ones,' he said, thinking of the children, 'should visit her again some time with a bunch of lilies. Your late mother, my heavenly one,' he smiled at Lakmé, 'and her sweet-jellied carp in the foreign style. Well, perhaps she can see us now, perhaps she's here. Perhaps she really came when I lit the candles and is now standing by the tree over there. But perhaps she's in a different body now. We mustn't be so conceited as to believe that she is no longer reincarnated, that she has reached her goal already. That's very rare; some pharaohs, saints, one of the Dalai Lamas . . .' Mr. Kopfrkingl glanced towards the bookcase, smiling. 'And what may Mr. Míla Janáček be doing, my lovely,' he smiled at Zina. 'He's having dinner with his parents and thinking of you. He gave you a nice present and sent a nice Christmas card. He's a good boy, he's fond of music, physics and machines. He's from the best family and deserves happiness in his life. And what about the young Misses Lenka and Lála, your fairhaired classmates? The Bettelheims,' Mr. Kopfrkingl looked at Mili, 'are also having a feast now. They celebrate Christmas like us. I don't think they've ever observed any Jewish festivals. At the same time, he comes from a distinguished Hungarian Jewish family, that good noble philanthropist of ours, Dr. Bettelheim. He invited me up to his surgery once and told me that,' he said with a glance at the picture of the wedding procession by the window. 'He told me that in connection with the beautiful old picture he's got hanging on the wall there. It depicts the abduction of a woman by Count Bethlén which failed . . .' Mr. Kopfrkingl looked round the walls of the dining-room . . . then he stared at the ceiling as if he was seeing the starry sky, and then he glanced at

Mili again and said: 'And what may the Prachařs be doing? Poor Mrs. Prachař, I haven't seen her for a long time now; poor Vojta Mr. Prachař's son.'

New carols could be heard on the radio. Mr. Kopfrkingl gazed at the Christmas tree for a while and then at the cat, who came up to him, and then he said:

'It's Christmas Eve, my dears, and the Temple of Death is idle today. Today it's deserted and empty. Even Mr. Dvořák is not there, nor Mr. Vrána in the porter's lodge, who sits there because he's got something wrong with his liver . . . even Mr. Fenek with the nail on his little finger isn't in the porter's lodge. He's *somewhere* at home. I wonder how he is spending his Christmas Eve . . .? And what may Mrs. Strunný and Miss Čárský be doing . . .?' he said, listening to the radio on which "Sweet Was the Song the Virgin Sang" could now be heard. 'If they were in the ground they'd look horrifying now, poor things . . . luckily they're not in the ground but are dust in the urn and their souls are undergoing further reincarnation. There are only a couple of corpses lying in the preparation room in the Temple of Death today, waiting for the festival to finish. Christmas Eve is not a day of death but of birth,' he said with a glance at the radio on which "While Shepherds Watched" could now be heard, 'and so there's no cremation. Just like Saturday afternoon,' he smiled at Mili, 'there's no cremation on Saturday afternoon either . . . But there should be one on Christmas Eve. Precisely because Christmas Eve is a day of birth. There should be many funerals on such a joyous day so that as many souls as possible could extricate themselves, free themselves, fly up into the universe, and find new bodies. Christmas Eve should be generous to the dead as well. At least these dear fried carp will get something out of it . . .' he added. On the radio, they had just begun singing "God Rest You Merry Gentlemen".

When they had finished the fried carp, Mr. Kopfrkingl put the newspaper and a bottle of wine on the table. "Come All Ye Faithful" was on the radio. They filled and then clinked their glasses, though he only wetted his lips. 'Just symbolically,' he said, 'I'm abstemious. On the other hand, I'm also a pure Germanic soul. Yes . . .' he smiled at Lakmé, who glanced up, 'Willi told me that today. Predestined, chosen,' he smiled towards the glass. 'He and Erna are having dinner in the German Casino today. The Casino is in Růžová Street. It's got a white marble-covered entrance with three steps. Willi's having dinner in high society. In case I should forget,' he smiled at Lakmé, who looked saddened somehow, 'the newspaper is full of accidents again. A woman committed suicide, allegedly because of hunger.' He looked at the newspaper and read out the news item and then read another piece: '"Mad dog bit five-year-old girl. Yesterday afternoon, a dog, belonging to Karl B. in Loučeň, broke loose from its kennel, ran out of the door onto the path where children were playing, and . . ." And here's something else,' Mr. Kopfrkingl gave a smile. 'I'd completely overlooked it, an advert. *Drapes and curtains repaired,*' he read, to the accompaniment of the children's chorus singing "Little Jesus, We Will Rock You" . . .' *by Josefa Brouček, Prague-Hloubětín, 7 Kateřinská Street.* . . in case I should forget,' he smiled at Lakmé. 'The curtain over there is giving trouble. We'll put it right before we start giving presents, so that our fiat will be flawless and without blemish – like paradise.'

Lakmé got up and went to the window. Mr. Kopfrkingl put aside the newspaper, took his chair and put it close by the curtain. Lakmé got up on it, and adjusted the cord, standing on the tips of her toes a little. 'It's working,' Mr. Kopfrkingl gave a smile after he had helped Lakmé jump down and checked the curtain. Then he embraced Lakmé and stroked her white lace collar.

'So,' he said, 'and now we are going to bring out the sweets for those who have a sweet tooth and give presents. Not every family has as many presents at Christmas as we do. There's still a great deal of poverty in our country and in the world. Willi also told me today,' he gave a smile, 'that everything depends on the ability to see the whole. To think about the future. About a better life for our children and for those who will follow after us. About a happier life for mankind. So, it seems to me,' Mr. Kopfrkingl smiled somewhere in the direction of the bookcase, 'that Willi spoke like a book . . .'

Then the radio began to play and sing "Jesus Christ, Our Saviour Was Born". Mr. Kopfrkingl brought out the presents which he had hidden in the living-room. Lakmé got stockings, an enormous jar of sweet-smelling cream with a golden and black label and a box of chocolates. Zina got a handbag, a box of chocolates and a piano score from Chopin's "Funeral March". Mili got a basket of chocolate rings, a little white car with a red cross, and a black pillow adorned with golden and silver tassels. And also an adventure book called "Death in the Primeval Forest".

X

'Willi only gave me the parcel in February and look, he's written to me today,' said Mr. Kopfrkingl to his darkhaired Lakmé, Zina and Mili in the dining-room three months after Christmas. 'Well, then, I'm going to do it in the room I like best in the flat, the bathroom, and I won't come out until I have completely finished. *My enchanting ones*,' he said, thinking of them all, 'don't knock on the door and don't call me, so that I'll be able to concentrate. Stand right away from the door so that you won't get a fright when I come out. The first impression will probably be shattering.' They all nodded rather uncertainly, even fearfully. Mr. Kopfrkingl took the parcel and disappeared into the bathroom.

'Ever since I came back from that good Dr. Bettelheim of ours, I've been constantly asking myself the question why on earth does that Hitler persecute the Jews so much in Germany?' said Mr. Kopfrkingl to himself in the bathroom, glancing at the beautiful white bath, at the white glossy ventilator where the cord was hanging on the hook, and at the yellow butterfly on the wall. 'Why does he persecute them so much? After all, they're such nice, kind and selfless people. Well, now I know why. Willi explained it to me. He's persecuting them because they're against him. Because they're against the German nation. Because they are a wretched, erring people who don't understand . . .' Mr. Kopfrkingl hung his head sadly and untied the parcel.

The trousers were mouldy and threadbare; the jumper dark, ugly and full of holes. The shirt was hideously dirty at the neckline. 'Willi warned me against washing,' Mr. Kopfrkingl gave a smile. 'He said that beggars never wash their clothes. They walk around wie eine Schlampe.' The greyish overcoat was narrow and shiny with broken buttons dangling from it. 'Willi recommended,' Mr. Kopfrkingl gave a smile, 'that I don't button it up. Beggars leave it unbuttoned so that others can see what they have on underneath. A jumper full of holes and a dirty shirt . . . Willi didn't give me anything for my head to set off this wig . . .' He took out a wig made of tousled grey hair. It was bald on the crown, with yellowish overlapping shocks of hair round the ears. 'No combing,' smiled Mr. Kopfrkingl, 'the beggars walk around, Willi said, den ganzen Tag wie sie vormittags aus dem Nest kriechen.' Then he took a pair of bushy eyebrows out of the parcel and two pale yellow strips of disgusting stubble, the kind that can be stuck on the face from the hairline, alongside the ears, towards the cheekbone. They were in a celluloid case with a 'Made in Germany' label. Then he took out a jar containing three different kinds of greasepaint. . . 'Ah, this is the greyish white one, the dirty

one, as Willi said,' Mr. Kopfrkingl gave a smile. 'Here's the
rosy one, for the complexion, and this is the bluish one, or
the consumptive, cold one. It's supposed to be the most
difficult thing of all to put grease-paint on your skin. Once
it's on I'm supposed to dry it as women do theirs with
powder-puffs. Mit einem Puderzeug... Here are the specs,'
Mr. Kopfrkingl carefully took out the specs. 'It's a miserable pair of half lenses, half a dioptre each, on twisted wire
frames. Willi doesn't recommend plain glass for false spectacles. And here's some miraculous stuff. Eine Wundermate-
rie. Willi said to warm it up a little like wax, *like wax* . . .,'
Mr. Kopfrkingl gave a smile and passed his hand, on which
something flashed, over his forehead . . ., 'to make a bump
for my nose. It'll change it beyond recognition. It's a grey-
white-ochre colour, the dirty complexion one. It hasn't got
any violet in it which one usually sees in drunkards. Willi
said that alcoholic beggars arouse disgust rather than pity,
and I mustn't do that. A professor allegedly established that
in a survey in Berlin . . . But that's good,' Mr. Kopfrkingl gave
a smile. 'After all, I don't actually drink, myself. I don't drink,
I don't smoke, I'm abstemious,' he smiled into the mirror.
'Poor Mr. Prachař from the third floor. . . And, then last of
all, there's this pair of lace-up shoes with the loose soles.'

Mr. Kopfrkingl made sure that he had locked the bathroom door properly and began changing his clothes and
disguising himself. 'Oh yes, where am I going and why,' he
smiled into the mirror once he had put on the mouldy trousers and shirt, and the thought flashed through his mind
why he was going and where, what Willi had told him . . .
'Nothing strange,' Willi had laughed in the dining-room last
February when he had brought the parcel along. Neither
Lakmé nor the children were at home then. 'There's a disguise in this parcel. A beggar's disguise. You'll put it on on
the sixth of March and go to our Casino in Růžová Street
first; you know, to that white marble-covered entrance

with the three steps. I'll meet you there at half past four, stop you, *give you a twenty-heller coin* and tell you quietly whether you're changed beyond recognition. From the Casino you'll go slowly to Maislova Street, to the Jewish Town Hall, and stay there for a while. Why?' Willi had given a laugh, 'Nothing strange about it. On the sixth of March the Jews are holding a celebration in the Town Hall in Maislova Street at six o'clock in the evening. You'll stay there in front of the entrance for a while, vor dem Ausgang, vor dem Tor. You could read the glass plate that's by the entrance while you're there; you know, there's a sort of glass plate hanging beside the entrance to the Town Hall . . . as it happens, there's a street lamp nearby, so you can easily pretend to be reading it at six o'clock in the evening. Well, then you'll go home again. You'll open the door as carefully as when you went out, and change back into your usual skin; Mr. Kopfrkingl, employee of the Prague crematorium. That's all. It'll be a kind of test of your strength and courage, so eine vortreffliche Exerzierung, or to put it more clearly, it'll be a way of helping these poor, lost, erring Jews, who oppose the well-being and happiness of our people. How can this help them? I'll tell you later, when we meet in Růžová Street in front of the Casino on the sixth of March . . . I hope you're interested in it,' Willi added. 'You've always been against violence and war, against exploitation, poverty and suffering. Besides, you are, after all, employing two Jews as agents, a Mr. Strauss and a Mr. Rubinstein, two decent, good, orderly people. Why shouldn't you help them? Does the meaning of your life consist of forever regulating the flow of coffins into the furnaces?' And then, after a moment of silence, Willi dived into his pocket and handed his friend Kopfrkingl a piece of paper. 'This is an *application form* for membership of the SdP,' and he gave him the form. 'There's still time, join the party. It's high time you did. Look here,' he said as he was on the point of leaving, glancing at the picture of the Nicaraguan president above the door, 'that clown's still hanging up here ... a perfect print of a perfect gentleman would be just right here. The portrait of the Führer and Reich Chancellor, not this clown ...' And Willi took his leave and went. That was in February, Lakmé and the children had not been at home then, and it was now the sixth of March. Mr. Kopfrkingl stood in the locked bathroom. He already had the mouldy trousers and the shirt on. He completed his diguise and then ... he looked into the mirror and nearly shuddered at what he saw.

It was not he, Mr. Roman Kopfrkingl, the husband of his heavenly one and the father of his two beautiful ones, standing here in the bathroom. It was a completely different person who stood there, a real beggar, eine menschliche Ruine ...

'An old beggar whom I've never seen or known in my life,' said Mr. Kopfrkingl to himself. 'How completely one can change, be transformed ... and with what? With Willi's disguise ...' Then he said to himself: 'My lovely ones are standing by the window in the dining-room and waiting, waiting for me ... while I ... when I open the door and go in ... in fact, I won't go in at all! It'll be this one ...,' he pointed to himself in the mirror, 'this one ...' Then he said to himself: 'I hope they won't get too big a fright. I hope I won't shock them too much. I mustn't shock them too much, I mustn't,' he said to himself in front of the mirror, glancing at the ventilator with the cord on the hook and at the yellow butterfly underneath. 'They're much too dear to me to get a big fright ...' Then he finally tore himself away from the mirror, and raised his eyes to the ventilator as if begging heaven for strength, when a thought occurred to him: 'If that Mr. Fenek of ours could see me now, poor thing. Or Mr. Dvořák...' Then he went to the door, put his hand on the door handle but, at the last moment, remembered that, in order to enhance the disguise, Willi had recommended that he drag his left leg behind him a little, den Fuss ein wenig nach-schleppen . . . and to bend forward slightly . . . He bent his trunk slightly, got his leg ready for dragging and went out. . .

He first glimpsed but a fraction of the scene in the din-ing-room: – Lakmé's fingers on her slightly opened lips by the standard lamp, Zina's astonishment and Mili's stare, the cat's as well. He stood for a while on the threshold, with his leg behind him and his body bent forward, under the picture of the Nicaraguan which was still hanging there. Then he took two steps towards them, towards Lakmé, Zina and Mili, and the cat. And then, lowering his voice and extending his hand with the palm up, he bleated:

'Good people. Have you got a little piece of bread? I ha-ven't eaten all day. Have you no mercy?'

It was terrible.

Zina was the first to rouse herself. She exclaimed:

'Father, you've forgotten to take your ring off.'

Indeed. Mr. Kopfrkingl's wedding ring sparkled on his left hand.

'Such a little thing, and how it could betray me,' Mr. Kop-frkingl gave a smile and straightened up. 'I must say how very pleased I am with you, Zina, my little one. I must take my ring off. It'll be the first time in my life, as you know, my dear,' he turned to Lakmé standing by the standard lamp. 'I haven't taken it off for one single moment in the nineteen years of our marriage . . .' And he gently slipped the ring off his finger, went up to the anxious Lakmé by the standard lamp, took her hand and tenderly put his ring into it. 'Watch over it, my dear, and look after it like the apple of your eye, like my own heart, so that I'll be able to take it from your pure hand and put it on again, this symbol of our faithful-ness and love, when I come back from my errand . . . May I kiss you, even as a wretched beggar?'

Lakmé embraced him and wanted to kiss him but he held back a little at the last moment.

'Just a token, my dear, a little kiss,' he gave a smile, 'so as not to disturb the grease-paint or upset the bump on my nose. When I come back I'll make it all up to you . . .'

Lakmé stepped back, she was still rather anxious, and said at last:

'Why are you doing it, Roman? Walking out onto the street like that. What is it for? And where are you supposed to go?'

'To the German Casino, my dear,' Mr. Kopfrkingl gave a smile, and also smiled at Zina, Mili and the cat. 'Willi's going to meet me there by the entrance at half past four, and then I'll go to Maislova Street in the Old Town. It's something to do with the Jews, my dear,' he smiled tenderly. 'I'm sure you'd understand that . . . but it would be a longish explanation . . .' he gestured slightly and then said: 'The question is, how to help them in some way. They're an unhappy, erring people. They fight against Hitler, the German nation. They don't know what they're doing . . . This is a kind of test of my strength and courage, a kind of exercise. Anyway, I'm going to tell you everything when I come back, don't worry . . . Zina, dear,' blinking behind the miserable specs, Mr. Kopfrkingl involuntarily touched his shock of hair. 'But Zina, dear, you were supposed to go out. It'll be four o'clock now. When were you supposed to meet?'

'At half-past three,' said Zina.

'At half-past three, my God,' exclaimed Mr. Kopfrkingl, 'the good Míla must be gone by now . . .' but Zina shook her head.

'What trust in people,' blinked Mr. Kopfrkingl and again involuntarily felt his shock of hair. 'He's a wonderful boy, that Míla. Well, run along and give him our kind regards. I'll leave the flat in five minutes.'

'Youth, oh youth,' Mr. Kopfrkingl smiled into the little mirror hanging in the dining-room after Zina had left. 'We weren't any different, Lakmé. It's already nineteen years since we met in the zoo in front of the leopard,' he smiled into the little mirror. 'The leopard has been called to meet his Maker long ago . . . But now I'll be going. Time flies, and I mustn't forget my duties. We must take care that nobody sees me leaving the flat. When I come back, my heavenly one, I'll make it all up to you, like God . . .' Mr. Kopfrkingl stroked Lakmé, who was still anxious and bewildered, and smiled at the cat and Mili, who was standing in the corner gaping. Then he bent forward, turned his leg aside, blinked at the picture of the Nicaraguan president above the door and went out into the hall. He blinked at Maryborough above the shelves for shoes, then listened for a while at the door and peered through the peephole. Then he turned round and said to Lakmé and Mili, who were trembling behind him, that there was nobody there, that everything in the house was quiet. He opened the door quietly and stepped outside.

As he went down the stairs, bent forward and holding the banisters, he wondered what would happen if somebody had seen him come out of his door after all. Perhaps they would think that Mrs. Kopfrkingl welcomed beggars in her flat. 'If the good Dr. Bettelheim should see me, for example, whom I visit in secret to check I'm not infected,' he thought, going down the stairs, bent forward and holding the banisters. 'What if it had been him of all people who'd seen this disgusting beggar leaving Kopfrkingl's flat? Or his beautiful elderly wife, or their nephew, Jan, or their housekeeper, Anežka, in her red apron, the loyal good soul . . .' Then he found himself almost on the ground floor . . . and his heart nearly stopped. Mrs. Prachař, whom he hadn't seen in the house for such a long time, had just come in, Vojta beside her. Respectfully, he made way for them, stepping back against the wall . . . they passed him with an astonished glance and may have even turned round to look at him . . . he dragged himself to the front door. 'They haven't recognized me,' he said to himself at the door. 'Of course, how could they? The disguise is excellent, how perfectly it can change one, transform one . . . poor Mrs. Prachař, poor Vojta, let's hope he won't inherit it from his father.' He stepped out onto the street and mingled with the people who were passing the apartment house. But still he turned to look round a little, and it seemed to him that Zina was hanging about in the distance, on the opposite pavement, watching. Further off a little terrier was answering the call of nature.

The German Casino in Růžová Street, to which Mr. Kopfr-kingl had dragged himself with his leg behind him and his body bent forward, had a white marble-covered entrance with three steps. 'I love white marble-covered entranc-es with three steps,' thought Mr. Kopfrkingl and slowly crossed the street to the pavement opposite. 'They look like the entrance to some rich man's villa. They could even be the entrance to some grand ceremonial hall. Willi's in-side,' he thought. 'Willi's in there. I've never been inside, but I know it from his description. The carpets, mirrors, pictures . . . lavatories, bathrooms . . . first-class Prague German society, deputies, factory-owners, professors from the German University, not all of them of course . . . Mr. Boehrmann, who frequently goes to Berlin to consult with ministers, and first-class waitresses, barmaids and hostess-es . . .' Mr. Kopfrkingl reached the pavement opposite and in-voluntarily leaned against the wall of a building . . . Then he peered through his specs, shifted his leg slightly and bent his body so that Willi would find him in the correct posture when he came out of that white entrance with the three steps. As he stood in this manner against the wall of the building opposite and gazed at the white entrance, several people passed by without him noticing them at all. Except for one woman. She was slim and had biggish breasts. She was a complete stranger, he had never seen her before in his life. She dived into her handbag, and before Mr. Kopfrkingl could recover himself, he found a twenty-heller coin in his hand. He did not even realize that a split second before he had extended his hand with the palm turned upwards as he had done when he came out of the bathroom at home. His heart nearly stopped at this gift. 'What a beautiful, good woman,' he thought when he roused himself from his astonishment. 'What proof that my disguise is perfect . . .' At that very moment he saw his friend Willi walking energetically towards him from the Casino's entrance.

'Fantastic,' Willi laughed, glancing after the woman, who was already far away. 'Fantastisch, tadellos. Why, you're completely changed. You're acting it just *like Chaplin*. Come, let's walk together a little bit,' he gave a laugh, 'nebeneinander . . .'

With his leg behind him and his body bent forward, Mr. Kopfrkingl walks slowly beside Willi and says with a glance at Willi's elegant coat:

'Won't it attract attention – you walking with me?'

'Why?' says Willi. 'Why shouldn't a citizen of this republic walk with a beggar for a little bit? After all, *this is* a free, democratic country, isn't it? Ausgezeichnet,' he laughed with a glance at the feet, 'du schleichst wie ein echter Bettler.' Then Willi put his hands into the pockets of his elegant coat, lowered his head and said quietly:

'You want to live up to your honour. You were born for big tasks,' he smiled at the bluish face, shocks of hair and stubble beside him. 'You're getting along fine. You're doing it brilliantly. You're no weakling, you're a one hundred-percent man, with a pure German soul. Just *crawl* along the streets for a while to reinforce your inner resolve, and then off to Maislova Street. If you *shuffle* along there before six, it'll be the right time. Hang about the entrance, stick your hand out too. *Gape* at the plate by the gate. I told you, there's a kind of little glass plate hanging by the entrance, you can read it, there's a street lamp nearby . . . And then . . . try to catch . . . a few words. Einige Worte auffangen. A few words, the kind people usually say when going inside. Nämlich,' Willi gave a laugh, 'what Jews say when they enter the Jewish Town Hall on 6 March 1939, on Chevra sude, which is a festival. . . I'll ask tomorrow.' Then he said:

'You know that they're a wretched people who don't understand anything. They're so ancient, they're senile . . . But you can help them,' he said, 'help them when we find out what they're talking about, what their views are. Besides, this is nothing but a sort of little test for you, a training of sorts, as I told you at your place. Considering that you've been a member of the SdP since last month it's necessary to undergo a little such training. The whole German nation has undergone training, much more difficult training, in uniforms, in the field, in sacrifices . . . the young people in the Hitler Youth in boxing. What's all this *crawling* . . .?' Willi jerked his head at his friend Kopfrkingl creeping along beside him. 'Why, it's just plain tomfoolery compared to that. Well, and you'll also have to come to the Casino soon . . .'

Mr. Kopfrkingl smiled kindly, if it is at all possible to smile kindly in such a miserable beggar's disguise, and said:

'Beautiful carpets, pictures, bathrooms, you say . . . beautiful women?'

'Beautiful women,' Willi gave a laugh, '*fantastic!* You won't find more magnificent, affectionate women anywhere in Prague, und doch die Eleganz! Look here, those Petites of yours from the Malvaz pub, those Liškas, Strunnýs, Čárskýs of yours, or whatever you call them . . . you've got to put a stop to that. You won't need it. Does the meaning of your life consist of regulating the flow of coffins into furnaces and measuring temperatures for ever?' Then he said:

'You were born for big tasks, and so you'll have to keep company with suitable people. Go to Maislova Street, to the

Town Hall, to those erring ones, strain your ears. Today you shuffle there as a beggar, but one day you may go there in a Mercedes. In a beautiful, *green military* car . . . Well, go now, I'll ask tomorrow. Geh . . .'

Willi Reinke left and Mr. Kopfrkingl said to himself:

'He didn't even give me the twenty-heller coin he was to pretend to give me. It wasn't necessary. This amazing business makes me feel almost feverish. It's more amazing than the silver casket. It's just as interesting and strange, this change of mine, this transformation, as the Dalai Lama's reincarnation in my book about Tibet, although it's got nothing to do with it at all. Why, mine is just an ordinary kind of disguise, nothing more. If Mr. Fenek should see me now, poor thing. Or poor Mr. Dvořák,' he recalled again, 'but that doesn't matter. My forehead is as cool as metal, my hand is firm and my heart's beating as if it was made of Germanic steel. That's the test!' And steely calm and in disguise, he mingled with the poor unfortunate people in the street . . .

There was a blue Tatra saloon car parked in front of the Jewish Town Hall in Maislova Street, and Mr. Kopfrkingl began hobbling towards it as best as he could. He saw the lighted lamp, the glass plate behind it and the entrance next to it. 'What a sorry entrance,' he thought to himself, hobbling as best as he could. 'There's neither a trace of marble nor steps here, only grey plaster and a black metal-plated gate. Well, of course, it isn't the German Casino, it's the Jewish Town Hall . . .' For a while he hung around the Tatra car, gazing through his specs at its blue colour, looking right and left, his face assuming an expression of helplessness . . . Some people were going into the Town Hall and noticed him. 'I have to go to that plate by the entrance,' he said to himself and dragged his leg to the plate by the entrance. He touched his spectacles and, without straightening up, began to read:

'A feast,' whispered Mr. Kopfrkingl with one leg behind
him. 'The anniversary of both the birth and death of Moses.
He was born on *the same day he died*. What an absurdity.
What a myth . . .' he gave a smile, and then smiled again
and said to himself: 'The *Burial brotherhood* hall! What can
the Burial brotherhood be like, and what can the hall look
like? Carpets, mirrors, pictures . . . bathrooms . . . like the
Casino . . .' he gave a smile. 'They're certainly not going to
have those. It'll be probably something like our preparation
room in the crematorium or the funeral hall, without the
cross of course.' And he told himself that these poor wretches did not have themselves cremated but went back to the
earth where it took twenty years, twenty years, before
they returned to the dust from which they came. He said to
himself: 'Even in this they have gone astray, they don't understand. What did Willi say? Such an ancient nation that
it's already senile . . .' Then he heard more people coming
towards him, turned round, lifted his shoulders slightly on
his bent body, and crouching even lower, raised his eyes
pleadingly from under his specs and held out his hand.

They came up to him, standing by the entrance, paused,
and dived into their pockets and handbags. Coins fall into
Mr. Kopfrkingl's hand, who trembles, peering through his

specs and twitching his leg. His lips bleat out words of thanks in a quavering voice . . . May God reward you for everything . . . when suddenly some familiar faces appeared before Mr. Kopfrkingl's eyes . . . of course! His heart nearly stopped beating for the second time. Why, it's Mr. Strauss and Mr. Rubinstein, his agents, to whom he gives half, nothing less, those two good, decent, orderly people. More coins fall into Mr. Kopfrkingl's hand. Poor things, they haven't got anybody, Mr. Kopfrkingl thinks to himself. Mr. Rubinstein is divorced, Mr. Strauss's wife died of consumption of the throat and his little son of scarlet fever. If they but knew to whom they gave . . . And then suddenly, standing in front of him is . . . yes, he nearly crumpled at the knees, it's him, Dr. Bettelheim, the consultant in skin and venereal diseases, from their apartment, that good noble philanthropist . . . 'Violence,' the thought flashes through Mr. Kopfrkingl's mind, 'rewards nobody for long. It can't make history . . . you can stun people, intimidate them, drive them under the ground, but for how long . . .? After all, we live in a civilized world . . .' Standing behind Dr. Bettelheim is his beautiful elderly wife. More coins keep falling into Mr. Kopfrkingl's hand . . . and here is their Jan . . . he is walking with his head cocked somehow as if he was listening to music . . . He hasn't the faintest idea, that good, nice boy, just like his uncle and aunt. If they only knew . . . but Anežka isn't with them, Anežka is a Christian, she has a red apron . . . It was all like a dream. And then they stopped coming, they were already inside, they were already in the Town Hail, and Mr. Kopfrkingl found himself alone in front of the entrance, alone with the blue Tatra car. He turned round to look at the plate once more and said to himself:

'Burial brotherhood, feast, participants will be treated to a meal: Moses was born and died on this day. What if I went in too? It's true, I'm not a Jew, I'm a pure Germanic soul, but I'm such a perfect beggar that they would, I'm sure, give me a plate. Jews will clearly give to such a wreck, as I saw for myself, even if the wreck is, as they say, a goy . . .' Mr. Kopfrkingl gave a smile, counted his money and found that he had six crowns. With the coin from the Casino it made six twenty. 'I've earned six twenty in this beggar's disguise,' smiled Mr. Kopfrkingl. 'Six from the Jews who went to Chevra sude, and twenty hellers from the Aryan woman . . . If Willi had also given me a twenty-heller coin in front of the Casino, I'd have six forty . . .' And then he left.

The streets were already dark, the lamps were all on . . . After he had shuffled his way to the Jindřišská Tower, he stopped in his tracks. 'Why, I didn't overhear a thing at the Jewish Town Hall,' he said to himself. 'Ich habe kein Wort aufgefangen. Why, I only heard myself, my words of thanks, my own bleating! What am I going to say to Willi when he asks tomorrow?' he said to himself. 'I ought to say something to Willi. I've always performed my duties punctiliously, and this was a kind of test, training; I've been a member of the SdP since last month. What if I told him that, while they were going into the Town Hall, they were saying: Hitler is a murderer; Goebbels is a criminal; that Mr. Boehrmann, the one from Prague who frequently goes to see the ministers in Berlin, is a monster, who will be destroyed, liquidated . . .' Mr. Kopfrkingl smiled sadly and shook his head. 'That probably wouldn't help those poor, erring, superannuated people, who don't understand,' he shook his head sadly. 'Rather the reverse, I'd say. Hitler would then persecute them,' he said to himself, 'even more . . .' Then he said to himself: 'I'll have to think of something else.'

Then the thought of his wedding ring, which he had left in the hand of his darkhaired beauty at home, caressed him. She seemed to be dejected and uneasy, and he started running. Behind the tower, at the crossroads with its passing trams and cars, he came across a young pink-faced girl in her black dress, walking arm-in-arm with a young man. He noticed her only briefly as he passed, and went on running. Then he came across an elderly woman in spectacles. She probably lived somewhere nearby because she was carrying a jug of beer . . . Then, behind the crossroads, he came across a little old fat man in a stiff white collar with a red bow tie. He was counting some cards with the fingers of one hand, the other he held with fingers clenched . . . He went on running, but slowed down for a while at the corner of one of the streets; a real beauty was standing under the lamp. He noticed that she had fair hair; he could overhear her telling somebody whom he could not see very well: 'Some people take soda water, some take ice . . .' Then he recalled the Casino again, and began to run as fast as he could on his loose soles.

XI

A week after the dinner in the Jewish Town Hall, the 15th of March came and with it everything that happened on that day and has been happening since. The *armed* forces of the Reich poured into the country. The Führer came to Prague. The flag of the Reich flew over Prague castle, over the houses, and possibly over the crematorium as well . . . and Mr. Kopfrkingl . . . Mr. Kopfrkingl might well have been standing about on the Prague streets during the moments he was not at his place of work, watching the army and reading the German inscriptions over the shops. He might even have gone to Ovocný trh to read the inscription over Mr. Kádner's bookbinder's shop, and to Nekázanka Street to read the inscription over Mr. Holý's picture-framing shop. But he definitely went to Růžová Street, quite often, to enjoy, at least from the pavement opposite, the Casino's white marble entrance with its three steps which reminded him of a rich man's villa, or a particularly grand ceremonial hall, or a palace of breathtaking mysteries, like a silver casket . . .

And then, in April, at the time of the Führer's birthday, he was at last honoured with an invitation to that Casino.

He was sitting there, in the luxurious hall with carpets, chandeliers, mirrors and pictures, with his friend Willi Reinke, the top official of the Prague Sicherheitsdienst, and his wife, Erna. She had a well-tended coiffure and biggish earrings. He was also sitting there with officers and officials, but not only them. There were excellent waitresses, barmaids and hostesses, fairhaired beauties. Mr. Kopfrkingl was in raptures over their beauty, warmth and elegance, in raptures over everything he had seen and heard, as well as over the food he was eating and . . .

'No thank you, I won't have a drink. Why . . .' he smiled at the ladies and gentlemen at the table, 'I'm abstemious. I don't smoke either. Willi and Erna know all about it. I feel sorry for Mr. Prachař from our apartment house, he's an alcoholic. His son, Vojta, could inherit it from him. It's a perversion. Such weak people are a burden, they cannot contribute to the battle for tomorrow. Of course, this is something else,' he said quickly, pointing to the glasses on the table. 'This isn't alcoholism. But then, we mustn't suspect and judge others without reason, we have faults enough of our own. There are some beautiful mirrors and pictures here,' he smiled into the hall. 'I'd say this place is like *paradise*. The whole world should look like this in the coming, happy and just order,' he gave a smile, finally fixing his gaze on the fairhaired beauties.

'It'll be within our power,' Willi gave a smile, 'in our power if we all perform our duties. It depends on each one of us,' he repeated, 'on each one of us, if wars, poverty, hunger, disrupted families, ruined marriages, as you say . . . exploitation and suffering are to disappear from this world,' Willi gave a smile. 'Why shouldn't it be possible in this life? Why should it be only in the life eternal? . . . Can you see anybody suffering here now . . .?' Willi spread his arms and glanced at the blondes, who burst out laughing, Erna did too. 'See, nobody's suffering here, and if it's possible here and now, in the German Casino in Prague, why shouldn't it be possible everywhere else, and for ever, in Warsaw, Budapest, Paris, Brussels, London, New York . . .? But the Führer will have to win through first. As soon as he has won through it'll be like this everywhere, and not even horses will suffer . . .' Willi leaned towards his friend Kopfrkingl and gave a laugh. 'The armed forces of the Reich,' he gave a laugh, 'don't need horses as the Austrian army did in the days of the War. The armed forces of the Reich are *mechanized, automated* . . . But we have enemies, mein lieber Karl,' said Willi.

'Every great achievement is born out of the opposition put up by the enemy,' said Willi. 'You have to expect that. People are people, not angels, and evil, as you say, is committed by people . . . The Führer has eliminated one bastion of war, this former Republic, but it doesn't mean that there aren't other evil-doers. That we can now rest on our laurels. That we can calmly close our eyes and go to sleep. Evil-doers may be hiding in all the social strata. They could be scientists, artists, writers . . . they could be former officers of the Czechoslovak army and the police, they could be priests . . . but they could also be ordinary cleaning women, mechanics, stokers, or businessmen and directors; people who set others at loggerheads, instigate, incite . . . and they're dangerous as long as we don't know about them. As long as we don't know about them, we can't transfer them to other places of work, take note of them, follow them . . . We'd be committing an offence against our German nation and mankind if we sat on our hands and just looked on at their destructive work . . . You're our only man in your workplace, in the crematorium, the only German, the only upholder of civilization and representative of the new order. And now a member of the NSDAP. We have to rely on you. Well, then, how do things look at your place . . .?' said Willi lightly, and Erna, the blondes, the officers and officials all fixed their eyes on Mr. Kopfrkingl. . .

'Well, then, how do things look at our place,' Mr. Kopfrkingl nodded his head thoughtfully, slightly pushing away the glass of wine which had been put in front of him . . . 'It's tragic . . . There are those people who don't understand anything. . . They're even worse now, after the fifteenth of March, unfortunately . . .' Mr. Kopfrkingl raised his head; he saw them all looking at him, and pushing his glass still further away . . . he said:

'Take Zajíc and Beran, for example. They're both enemies of the Reich and the new just order. Besides, they have already objected to the occupation of the Sudetenland. Vrána in the porter's lodge in the courtyard, who is there because he's got something wrong with his liver; I don't talk to him much, but his behaviour shows him to be rather unreliable, unfortunately. Mrs. Liška used to clean up for us at one time but has now left . . . I don't have her address, unfortunately, but we can find it out . . . Mr. Pelikán who opens the iron curtain in the funeral hall and lets people into the ether . . . but he's not bad, he's alright so far . . . On the other hand, the director, the director of the crematorium, of *my* Temple of Death,' he said, and Willi laughed with the others. He felt that he had risen in their estimation by making this comparison . . . 'Well, the director doesn't have the correct attitude towards the Reich either. I'd cremate all the Germans in these ovens, he said once, even after the fifteenth of March. His name is Srnec . . . I'm not sure whether he should go on being director . . .' he looked round, and Willi and the others nodded. He felt that they agreed with his objection, and Willi said:

'It seems out of the question that he should go on. We have no need to keep him there since you're there and are thoroughly experienced in these things . . . Karl Kopfrkingl, gentlemen,' Willi turned to the officers and officials, 'has been working in the crematorium for twenty years . . .' They all nodded, Mr. Kopfltringl smiled kindly, and then Willi said:

'And what about the people in your private life, those poor unhappy Jews of yours who are extremely dense – that superannuated race which is suffering from senility – you even employ two of them . . .' and Mr. Kopfrkingl shook his head and said:

'I know.' And then he pushed the glass of wine further away and said:

'Mr. Strauss, my agent, is a good, decent fellow. Sensitive, he's fond of music. He works well. We have to be fair in our judgements . . . But perhaps he works so well because he's only interested in gain. He's a commercial traveller in confectionery. He doesn't agree with the Protectorate and the Germans. He's against them. Mr. Rubinstein, the other one, is also a good, decent, sensitive fellow. He is fond of music too. He also works well, but probably also for gain. He used to be a representative in bed-linen. Well, and he doesn't like the Führer and the Reich . . . Who?' Mr. Kopfrkingl smiled at Willi's question and passed his hand over his forehead. 'Ah, Dr. Bettelheim from my apartment house. He's a good-natured fellow,' he passed his hand over his forehead. 'Of course, he doesn't understand either. He once maintained that the Germans commit acts of violence, and that violence cannot make history. People can only be silenced for a short time. We live, he said, . . .' Mr. Kopfrkingl looked round the ladies and gentlemen, 'in a civilized Europe in the twentieth century. . . Well, his wife doesn't like us either. Probably their nephew, Jan, is steeped in it as well. A very nice boy, he's fond of music . . . Their housekeeper, Anežka, is not Jewish, she's a good old soul, but she's apparently steeped in it as well. She killed the carp for us at Christmas. I wouldn't . . .' Mr. Kopfrkingl wiped his hands on a napkin, 'do it . . .' Willi nodded. He called his adjutant, or whoever it was, to the table. He had more wine brought to the table, cognacs as well, coffee for his friend Kopfrkingl, and lobster titbits and almonds. He also invited another beauty to join them.

'As we're talking about the Jews anyway,' Willi Reinke said, glancing at Erna and the other ladies and gentlemen at the table, 'you can see yourself now why the Führer doesn't like them. He doesn't like them because they don't understand. They're against us and spread their hatred of us. You say yourself that their housekeeper, Anežka, is not Jewish, but that she, too, is steeped, *steeped*, – that's the right word and why shouldn't she be? – to be sure. Why shouldn't she be? To be sure. Considering she's been living *with them* for years. They're an unhappy, erring people who don't understand us and won't do so, even in the future. Don't think that you can re-educate, persuade, convince them. They don't have the brains for it . . .' Willi pointed to his forehead. 'They're senile from old age. It's hereditary. Even when you stood as a beggar in front of the Jewish Town Hall last March you were ineffably superior to them. When you took off your beggar's outfit you became Karl Kopfrkingl again, the Teuton, the Aryan, of pure Germanic blood. On the other hand, when they took off their outer garments, they remained the same unhappy, miserable Jews. It's the same with music, as you say. There are people who are wretched because they die without ever learning of the beauty of Liszt or Schubert. These poor things, on the other hand, die without learning of the strength and beauty of the Greater German Reich. They suffered a great deal in the past, they were persecuted. Do you think they were persecuted for no earthly reason whatever? Have you ever heard about the *plague*?' Willi gave a smile and took a sip of cognac. 'That scourge of the Middle Ages which caused hundreds of thousands of people to die? What caused the plague, do you know?' Willi gave a smile, and

Mr. Kopfrkingl looked around at those present and fixed his gaze on Erna rather uncertainly, irresolutely . . . 'Well,' said Willi, 'poisoned wells. Why, the Jews poisoned the wells to exterminate the Christians. Didn't you know that? But we mustn't concern ourselves with the past or *origins*,' Willi waved his hand, laughing. 'What happened, happened. It's all past now. You maintain that we all come from the same dust and will return to the same earth, that there's no difference in human ashes. After all, you're an expert in it . . . And you should become the director. After all, the meaning of your life does not consist in regulating for ever the flow of coffins into furnaces and measuring temperatures. So, we're not interested in origins, but in results. Which are that the Jews are against the Führer, against us, against the Greater German Reich. They obstruct our happiness, endanger the Führer's European order, his mission, our position as the elect, which includes you. Only individuals seem to be good, your Mr. Strauss and Rubinstein for example. You always said that they were good, decent people, but you can see for yourself now that it's not so, that you've misjudged them: that Dr. Bettelheim too, whom you've always praised so much. Now you can see how he has incited and infected even his own nephew. Well, as far as that goes, there's no doubt that he's a relative – but he's also infected the housekeeper, who's not Jewish. In Sparta, ladies and gentlemen,' said Willi turning to those present, 'they used to kill their sickly children. It may seem cruel to some sensitive souls. But it was, after all, an act of immense kindness to those children themselves. How they would have suffered had they lived . . . and then, it was healthy for the nation. How greatly it contributed to Sparta's soundness and how successful was Sparta's history! We'd be committing an offence against the nation and mankind,' Willi turned to his friend Kopfrkingl, 'if we didn't get rid of undesirable elements. We're responsible for the happiness of the German nation and of the whole of mankind. For the prosperity of the whole. The details are a *mere decoration or complement*, nothing more.'

Willi lapsed into silence, as if he had just made a profoundly statesmanlike speech. At the table, the officers and officials were smiling and gazing at Mr. Kopfrkingl as if they had delivered the speech Willi had just made themselves. Mr. Kopfrkingl sipped his coffee and gazed at them too, at Erna and the two fairhaired beauties and also at the new one who had joined them a little while ago. She was as beautiful as an angel, and looked like a first-class actress. Then he looked around the hall a little, at the mirrors, the pictures . . . and Willi said:

'Mankind benefits by strength alone, but to do so it must be pure, healthy, incorruptible . . . have a drink,' Willi pushed the glass to his friend, and when he refused, took a swig himself with a smile and said: 'Weaklings can't accomplish anything. Show them your strength and you'll see. To associate with Jews is incompatible with German honour. Here . . .' With a sweep of his arm he took in the Casino, mirrors, pictures . . . 'There are only pure, one hundred-percent people. Champions of Teutonism destined to make a *sacrifice* in the interest of the new order . . . There are no Czechs or Slavs here . . . Listen, Karl . . .' Willi suddenly lowered his voice and looked at the others. . . 'your Marie's, your Lakmé's mother used to make sweet-jellied fish in the foreign style, as you said. Do you know what style it is? It's Jewish . . .' When Mr. Kopfrkingl looked a little startled, Willi said:

'Why, your Lakmé's mother was *Jewish*!'

Karl Kopfrkingl sat stock-still.

'Lakmé,' said Willi and took a drink, 'Your blackhaired Lakmé, in whom everyone can recognize it, once said when I reminded her of your German blood that you only speak Czech at home. Your blackhaired Lakmé was always greatly embarrassed and uneasy when I visited you and reminded you of your affinity to things German. Your Lakmé always maintained that *names don't matter* . . . Of course not, considering that her maiden name was *Stern*. Your Lakmé tried to conceal my invitation to the boxing-match from you; she had it tucked away *in the dresser next to the plates*. Of course she wanted to prevent you and Mili seeing the Führer's sport. She wasn't pleased when you joined the SdP last February, and it was high time you did, for the Führer came in March. The fact that you've always spoken Czech at home is not your fault, but hers, because she's Jewish. The fact that you didn't feel the German blood in you isn't your fault either, but hers. She tried to suppress it in you because she's Jewish. What she said when you went to Maislova Street as a beggar in March, I don't know. What she said when you were admitted to the NSDAP is something I'd rather not know. But I'd like to know what she's going to say when you start sending your children to German schools. I do know at least one thing today, and that is her unsuitable influence on Mili. That boy's so soft, almost feminine. Don't you see it? Of course, that's how they operate, on the quiet, corroding them, starting with children . . . I'd like to know what she would say if *you became* . . . may I . . .?' Willi Reinke suddenly got up, the others rising to their feet as well . . . 'May I introduce you . . .?'

'Herr Kopfrkingl, we thank you for services rendered,' the dignitary who had just arrived said harshly. 'You've got experience, you could put it to good use . . . As a thorough-bred German you can't be indifferent to . . . do you know what Anforderung an die Reinheit des Blutes means? I'm afraid that it wouldn't be possible for you to hold the high office which we want to give you, to carry out the honour-able mission you have taken upon yourself, *to become* . . . if in your own family there was . . . How long have you been married anyway, Mr. Kopfrkingl?' The dignitary gave a smile and motioned the others to sit down, himself sitting down as well . . . and Mr. Kopfrkingl . . .

'Our marriage has lasted nineteen years,' said Mr. Kopfrkingl. 'We met in the zoo, by the leopard, in the Predators' House. There's also a cage with a snake in that house,' he said. 'It's always seemed strange to me that they'd put the snake in there. It's still there, it's probably just a decoration, ornament, a mere complement . . .'

'Kopfrkingl,' nodded the dignitary, 'in the interest of the whole and of our mission we have to make *sacrifices*. I want to speak to Boehrmann, the chief of the Prague Sicherheitsdienst and secretary to the Reich Protector next week . . . But I fear what he's going to say . . . Indeed, I'm afraid that it would be impossible for you to hold such a high office under the circumstances . . .' The dignitary smiled at Erna and the blondes, and also at the one who looked like an angel and first-class actress. Mr. Kopfrkingl also smiled at Erna and the blondes. The one who looked like an angel and first-class actress suddenly leaned on his shoulder and then . . . Mr. Kopfrkingl said:

'After all, I can get a *divorce,* gentlemen.'

After they had left their chairs, Willi and Erna stopped with Mr. Kopfrkingl in front of a magnificent picture of a naked woman, which was hanging on the wall facing the side of the hall containing the bar with its cognacs and wines. The attendant handed the green Tyrolean hat with the braid to Willi, who said:

'Yes, it would be very sensible. To get a divorce. After all, you could remarry. *Once again*, don't you agree?' he said, glancing at Erna, and she gave a nod. 'But the main thing is that Lakmé should understand that she doesn't deserve to live with you, that it's incompatible with your honour . . . with the honour of a National Socialist. Do you remember how that Dr. Bettelheim of yours . . .' he said, glancing at the picture of the naked woman, 'was interested in her health once . . .? You told me so yourself. Of course, now I expect you understand. It's perverse, Karl,' he said and glanced at his green Tyrolean hat with the braid. 'Everything is perverse, perverse and nothing more. The weak and inferior, Karl . . .' Then he said:

'A lot of hardships are in store for her, Karl . . .'

He did not return home from the Casino until the early morning. They were all asleep. In the dining-room, where the Nicaraguan president was still hanging above the door and the chart on the black cord, the most sublime timetable and the picture of the wedding procession by the window, he gently repulsed the cat, who had woken up and come over to his legs . . . For a while he gazed at the family picture over the cabinet, then he took the book about Tibet out of the bookcase, seated himself under the standard lamp and began to read. Then his eyes began to close under the lamp and it seemed to him as if somebody was coming out of the book, which was slipping into his lap, some sort of mental fantasy. He went to bed.

XII

'We're here,' under the bushy green trees Mr. Kopfrkingl inhaled inconspicuously as if he wanted to purify his lungs secretly. 'We're here.' Then he stroked his hair which was stirred by a faint breeze, pointed upward and said:

'What a height. When we get up there we'll be sixty metres closer to the sky. But never mind,' he smiled at Lakmé in her dark dress with the white lace collar, at Zina in the black silk dress she got for her birthday, and at Mili in his beret, licking a choc-ice. 'Never mind. Great things are happening and we've got to understand them. If there are no sight-seeing flights, if we can't see Prague from a plane, at least we'll go up there and see it from sixty metres up. It's better to see Prague from a height of sixty metres than from nothing,' he said and thought inwardly, than from nothing or from ground level or *from an even greater depth*. Then he gave a nod and asked his dear ones to go inside.

They entered a round vestibule with a number of iron pillars. It was pleasantly cool inside. They entered the space between the metal railings and found themselves at a brick-built box-office. Behind the window was an empty beer-mug and beside it an elderly woman in spectacles, who was selling tickets with a bitter smile. Mr. Kopfrkingl bought the tickets and headed with his dear ones for the lift.

'Are we going up in the lift?' asked Mili uncertainly, finishing his choc-ice, and Mr. Kopfrkingl nodded. 'Yes, we are,' he said. 'You won't be frightened, will you? Why, it's nothing.' Then he glanced at Mili again and said:

'You were also frightened when we went to see Madame Tussaud's and at that boxing-match with Willi, though in the end you saw that it was nothing. What are you frightened of?'

The lift came down, opened, and a little old fat man in a stiff white collar and a red bow tie came out, took the tickets from Mr. Kopfrkingl, and Mr. Kopfrkingl went in with his dear ones. In the lift there was a little chair and a small mirror on the wall. 'It's nice in here,' Mr. Kopfrkingl gave a smile when the lift was set in motion. 'Such a nice little cage. If it had bars,' he smiled at Lakmé, who was standing beside him somewhat dejectedly, 'all it would need would be the leopard . . .' The lift came to a halt, the little old fat man in the stiff white collar and red bow tie opened the door, and Mr. Kopfrkingl and his dear ones came out onto a round gallery. The gallery had plate-glass windows, both plain and coloured. A lot of them were open, letting the breeze into the gallery. 'We are,' Mr. Kopfrkingl gave a smile, 'on the highest spot of our blessed city. In a while it'll seem as though we're standing on a high mountain and watching the world below us.'

Mili and Zina rushed to the glass, to the spot on the gallery which had a view of the main part of the city, of part of the Vltava River, the Old Town, the National Theatre, Vinohrady, . . . and Mr. Kopfrkingl and Lakmé took up a position behind them. On the left, to the north of the gallery, with a view of the Little Quarter, the Castle, the Cathedral of St. Vitus and Dejvice, stood a pretty young pink-faced girl in a black dress and a young man beside her . . . To the west, round the corner, on the opposite side of the gallery which could not be seen because of the lift in the centre, there was apparently a group of people. Noisy whispering could be heard coming from them.

'So, this is Prague,' said Mr. Kopfrkingl, averting his eyes from the young pink-faced girl in the black dress on the left. 'It's below us as though it were in the palm of one's hand. As if we were standing on a high mountain and watching the world stretched out below us. There's the Vltava, the Charles Bridge, the National Theatre,' he said. 'Those two towers, that's the Týn Church. The tower nearer to us is the Old Town Hall, the truncated one behind is the Powder Tower . . . Over there's the National Museum. Over there at the back, that large white modern building in Vinohrady, is the Church of Our Lord's Most Sacred Heart. Take a look, Mili,' he said to Mili, 'through this piece of glass . . .' and he pointed to the pane of yellowish smoked glass. As Mili took a look, he said: 'That little piece of glass is similar in colour to those we've got in the windows of our furnaces. The most sacred windows in the world because you can see straight through them into the workshop of God at the very moment the soul leaves the body and flies up into the ether. Let me see what that Prague of ours looks like through this glass,' he leaned over, took a look and then raised his head again and said: 'Indeed. That Prague of ours is beautiful.'

They took a few steps to the left, to the north, to the spot with the view of the Little Quarter, the Castle, the Cathedral of St. Vitus and Dejvice. The young pink-faced girl in the black dress and the young man, who had been there first, also took a few steps farther on, to the west, with the view of the stadium and Košíře. Round the corner, on the opposite side of the gallery which could not be seen, the group of people apparently took a few steps too because they could not be seen either. They were on the opposite side of the gallery again, round the corner, to the south. Only noisy whispering could be heard.

'So, over there are Hradčany, the Cathedral of St. Vitus,' Mr. Kopfrkingl pointed through the window which was wide open, 'the castle of Czech kings and presidents. Take a look through this piece of glass,' he said to Mili and pointed to the yellow piece of smoked glass. While Mili was looking he said: 'That light-coloured broad building over there, with those pillars on the left, and all the cars parked in front of it, is Černín Palace, the former Ministry of Foreign Affairs. Today it's the residence of the Reich Protector, Baron von Neurath. Can you see, my dear?' Mr. Kopfrkingl smiled at Lakmé, who was standing beside him somewhat dejectedly. 'Can you see the flag of the Reich flying over the Palace? *Our* flag of the Reich,' he smiled at Lakmé and then said to Mili: 'Take a look through the glass.'

'The Alps are over there,' a loud whisper could now be heard round the corner, on the opposite side of the gallery. 'Over there is Salzburg . . .'

'What are you talking about?' a man's furious voice answered. 'What Alps, what Salzburg?! Those aren't the Alps, that's a rock in Podolí. That's not Salzburg, that's Bráník! You're not in a cinema, you're on the lookout tower . . .'

Mr. Kopfrkingl put his hand out through the open window, waved it and said:

'There's a lovely mild breeze out there.' Then he gazed at the tower of St. Vitus Cathedral.

'Is Říp over there?' asked Mili and Mr. Kopfrkingl nodded. 'Yes, Říp,' he gave a nod, 'Říp where Čech, our ancestor, ascended according to the Czech legend. But it's only a legend,' he smiled and withdrew his hand from the open window, 'a myth, an absurdity. It's something like the day of both the birth and death of Father Moses on the sixth of March . . .' he smiled at Lakmé and glanced fleetingly at her black hair . . . 'The peaks in the distance over there beyond Říp are Krkonoše,' he said, 'and beyond them is the *Reich*.'

Then they took a few steps again, to the west, to the spot with the view of the stadium and Košíře. The young pink-faced girl in the black dress with the young man also took a few steps farther on, to the south, with the view of Smíchov, Bráník and Podolí. Round the corner, on the opposite side of the gallery, the group of people apparently took a few steps too because they were again on the opposite side, round the corner.

'Over there is Masaryk's stadium,' said Mr. Kopfrkingl, 'It's deserted and empty now. Deserted and empty like the courtyard of my Temple of Death early in the morning, before it starts operating. The stadium was swarming with people last year, the Sokol rally was taking place then. When will it take place again, I wonder . . .' Mr. Kopfrkingl gave a smile. 'I know it's no longer called Masaryk's stadium, it's been given a different name. What can you do?' he gave a smile. 'There are names which aren't always suitable, *even if they don't matter*, as you say . . .' he smiled at Lakmé. 'Perhaps it's called the Baldur von Schirach stadium now. Ah,' Mr. Kopfrkingl raised his head. It seemed to him that he could hear distant music through the open window. Then he pointed towards Strahov, to a street between the houses and a garden with a looming black spot, a *black* spot, which was moving slowly, very slowly, forward like a little snake. 'A funeral,' said Mr. Kopfrkingl and put his hand out through the open window, 'there's a funeral over there. Can you see, my divine ones . . . Can you see, my ethereal one,' he said to Lakmé. 'Take a good look . . . can you see? They're probably taking *her* to Malvazinky, there's a cemetery there. Poor thing, she'll be put underground . . .'

'I didn't know,' said Zina, 'that you can hear music from such a distance. That you can hear music from below right up here.'

'It's quiet, clear,' Mr. Kopfrkingl whirled his hand in the open window. 'That lovely mild breeze outside is blowing in our direction. When it blows in our direction you can hear it. Pity that we can't see,' Mr. Kopfrkingl withdrew his hand from the open window and shielded his eyes, 'the coffin more clearly. I can see only some undertakers and plumed horses . . .'

'It's like in Split over there,' a woman's voice could be heard round the corner, 'I can see the sea.'

'Stop jabbering, if you please,' hissed a man's voice. 'Why, you've never been there. This isn't Split, it's Hloubětín. You're not in a waxworks, you're on the lookout tower . . .'

Again they took a few steps to the left; Mr. Kopfrkingl, Lakmé and the children to the south, to the spot with the view of Bráník, Podolí, Smíchov. The young pink-faced girl and the young man also took a few steps farther on, to the east, with the view of the main part of the city. Round the corner, on the opposite side of the gallery, the group of people apparently took a few steps too. Mr. Kopfltringl said:

'Over there are Bráník, Podolí, and Smíchov in front of them. You can see the Smíchov Brewery from here, that building with the chimney. But I don't drink,' he said, 'I'm abstemious. That is Barrandov,' he pointed to the rock and shielded his eyes with his other hand for he was standing facing the sun at that moment. 'It contains fossils. Fossils so terribly old,' he smiled at Lakmé, 'that if they were still *alive they'd be senile* . . . All sorts of beetles, butterflies and trilobites,' he gave a smile and put his hand out against the sun through the open window. 'Take a good look, my heavenly one, don't be afraid. There's a lovely mild breeze out there,' and he waved his hand in the air, his ring flashing in the sun.

'And over there is Svatá Hora,' a woman's voice exclaimed round the corner. 'And that green church tower between those houses is Jerusalem, and over there, where the white clouds are, is paradise . . .'

'Don't be a fool, if you please,' a man's voice snapped at her. 'What Svatá Hora? That's Říp. What Jerusalem? Why, that's Bohnice. Bohnice, the lunatic asylum,' he hissed indignantly. 'If you don't stop it at once, so . . .'

'So, here we are again,' Mr. Kopfrkingl gave a smile when they all once again took a few steps to the left in the gallery, and Mr. Kopfrkingl once more found himself with his dear ones on the spot with the view of the main part of the city, of part of the Vltava, the Old Town, the National Theatre, Vinohrady . . . 'So, we're here again. As if we were standing on the highest mountain and watching the world stretched out below us. Beneath our feet . . .' Mr. Kopfrkingl gave a smile and then pointed again, and said:

'Over there are the National Theatre, and the National Museum, and that enormous white-tiled building in Žižkov is the Pension Institute . . . If only that dear Marin of ours over the door in the dining-room could see it. That dear Marin of ours who later became Pension Minister . . . Over there, somewhere behind those Týn towers, is Ovocný trh . . . Over there, behind the Powder Tower nearer to us, is Nekázanka Street . . . over there the Old Town Square, František, *the market place of Prague*, the *pillory* . . .' he pointed behind the glass, and the ring on his finger flashed . . . 'Over there, somewhere behind the Museum, is *Růžová Street* . . . and behind those two gilded onion-shaped domes, those two

sparkling ones . . . see, over there in Vinohrady . . .' he pointed and the ring on his finger flashed. 'Don't you know,' he
smiled at Lakmé, 'what it is? Why, that's the Vinohrady syn-
agogue, the biggest one in Prague. *You really didn't know it?*'
He smiled at her black hair. 'Have you never been there? . . .
Well, somewhere behind those gilded onion-shaped domes
is – my Temple of Death. We can't see it from here, unfortunately, because it's behind the hill. We can't see it from
here, unfortunately, but the main thing is that it's *there*.
Take a look through the glass, Mili,' he urged the boy.

'It's sorta wobbly here,' said the woman round the corner. 'Why, it's some sorta swing.'

'Don't be an idiot, nothing's wobbling here,' a man's voice
bellowed at her. 'Everything's made of iron here. You're not
at a fair, you're on the lookout tower.'

'Let's go over there again,' said Mr. Kopfrkingl and took a
step to the left, in the direction of the Castle, but not quite
that far. The pretty pink-faced girl in black and the young
man also took another step, in the direction of Strahov, but
not quite that far either. Mr. Kopfrkingl put out his hand
through the open window again.

'It's sorta swaying here,' said the woman round the corner. 'I can feel it. It's sorta swaying here. Suppose it falls
down!'

'What an idea! Obviously!' a man's voice snapped, 'Obviously! This thing's actually going to fall down precisely
at the moment you're here. It's held together for a hundred
years, but just today, when you're here, it's going to fall
down. I don't have such luck.' Then he hissed: 'Everything's
made out of iron here, not *of wax*, you idiot. You're not
watching a *boxing-match*! You're on the lookout tower!'

'Well, and over there,' said Mr. Kopfrkingl and pointed
with his hand, 'over there, the river curves round. There's
Hloubětín. There's Kateřinská Street somewhere . . .' he
said and pointed with his hand. 'We can't see it from here.

It's probably too small, I've never been there. I only know Kateřinská Street in Prague II.'

'Well, let's go a little farther still,' said Mr. Kopfrkingl after a while and took a few steps a little farther still to the left, towards the view of Hradčany. The pink-faced girl in black and the young man also took a few steps a little farther, in the direction of the stadium ... 'Hradčany again, the Cathedral of St. Vitus, the castle of Czech kings and presidents ... and that light-coloured, broad building with those pillars and all the cars parked in front of it, is Černín Palace, the former Ministry of Foreign Affairs, today the residence of Baron von Neurath, the Reich Protector. Can you see, my dear,' he smiled at Lakmé and put his hand through the open window, 'can you see the Reich flag flying over the Palace ... Take a better look, don't be afraid ...' he waved his hand, 'how mild the breeze is. How nice for the birds,' he glanced at Lakmé, 'to fly in it ...'

'I won't be able to go down,' the woman said loudly round the corner. 'I'd feel dizzy.'

'Who says you're going down, can you tell me?' snapped the man. 'You're going down in the lift.'

'What lift?' said the woman. 'What're you talking about? There isn't a lift going up and down. You're not in New York, you're in the *Reich*.'

'Will you kindly shut up,' the man shouted angrily and banged with something on the floor. 'Why shouldn't the lift be going up and down? Didn't you come up in it? Didn't it bring us up here? Did you *climb* up here on foot?'

'That funeral procession's gone now,' said Mr. Kopfrkingl after he had taken another few steps to the west, with a better view of Strahov. The pink-faced girl in black and the young man also took another few steps, to the south ... 'The funeral's gone now. That street between the houses and the garden, where the black spot was, is empty now. They're approaching the cemetery. But they're not going to

Malvazinky, they're probably going to Břevnov. Poor woman,' he said. 'Suppose it was a suicide.'

'How do you know, father,' said Zina, 'that it was a woman?'

'You can tell,' smiled Mr. Kopfrkingl, 'tell by feeling. Also by the music we heard before,' he gave a smile. 'Poor thing, it'll be a long time before she disintegrates. Twenty years at least. It would take her seventy-five minutes in the furnace.'

'I'll sprain my ankle and you'll get killed,' squealed the woman round the corner. 'There's a spiral staircase. You'd better pull your hat down over your ears or it'll fall off.'

'What're you jabbering about,' the man, now enraged, exclaimed and again banged with something on the floor so forcefully that it made a booming sound. 'I'm telling you there's a lift here, in this very spot . . .' he banged. 'You're going down in the lift just as you came up here, and that's that. And stop jabbering,' he shouted, 'or else. You know what's behind our backs? That Jerusalem of yours . . .' he said threateningly.

A grating sound could be heard in the centre of the gallery. The lift had just come up and two more visitors came out of the door. Then the little old fat man in the stiff white collar and the red bow tie came out and called out into the gallery:

'The lift's not going down, use staircase *two*,' and he shut the door with a click.

'There you are,' shouted the woman round the corner, 'There you are! What were you jabbering about? We're going on foot, you . . .' And then a woman in a hat with a long feather and a string of beads around her neck darted out from round the corner and ran, ran around the gallery. A fat little man in a bowler hat raced after her, with his stick raised. She ran round the gallery twice till everything shook and, in following her, he ran round twice too. Then she rushed off to staircase two and raced noisily down the stairs . . . The fat man took off his hat, took out his hand-kerchief and said to the people on the gallery:

'She's a fool. She saw Jerusalem and paradise from here. She thought she was in heaven up here. She does it to me all the time. I'm not going to take her anywhere any more.' He wiped his forehead with his handkerchief to the fading sound of vigorous steps flying down the staircase. 'She'll go to the lunatic asylum. Over there . . .' he pointed to Bohnice . . .

'Never mind, never mind,' said Mr. Kopfrkingl quickly when Mili turned to him and apparently wanted to say something, as perhaps did Zina and Lakmé, who was rather dejected. 'The lady probably felt dizzy. It can happen when you're *too high up*. But heaven can't be here,' he smiled sadly. 'That would mean that there'd be no suffering here, only angels. Then there'd be no death and no reincarnation either. *She*'ll get over it,' he said, 'she'll get over it once she's down there. *Down* . . .' Mr. Kopfrkingl glanced down at the sixty-metre drop and then pointed somewhere behind Dej-vice and said: '*Suchdol* is somewhere over there . . .' Then he turned round to look at the pretty pink-faced girl in black with the young man and said:

'Well, my ethereal ones, we'll be going too . . .'

They stepped out onto staircase *two* and began descend-ing slowly. Zina went first, in the black silk dress she had been given for her birthday, then Mili, holding the banister tightly with one hand and his beret with the other and walking at a snail's pace, followed by Lakmé, in her dark silk dress with the white lace collar, who held the banister too . . . and Mr. Kopfrkingl was last.

'It's as if the wall which surrounds us and obstructs our view,' he smiled at Lakmé's black hair in front of him, 'has collapsed at such a height. It's as if we were on the highest mountain with the whole world at our feet.' Then he said: 'Death is beautiful and precious, but we must make sure that cremation is carried out. Not like the poor woman whose funeral we saw in Strahov. The person who has made sure of cremation need be afraid of nothing. He can die without fear,' he smiled at Lakmé's head in front of him and then glanced down through the iron pillars at the slightly less than sixty-metre drop, for they were still at the top of the staircase. He put his hand out into the lovely mild breeze and said: 'It's just right for jumping.'

Below in the vestibule, by the railing near the box-office, the elderly woman in spectacles was picking up a broken feather and a broken string of beads from the floor.

XIII

'I couldn't get here in time,' said Mr. Kopfrkingl to Srnec, in a rather dry though not unkind manner, in the director's office a few days after his visit to the Casino and the lookout tower. 'Something unexpected has happened. I was holding a consultation.' The director glanced at Mr. Kopfrkingl and did not say a word. Not a muscle moved in his face, and neither did his eye. Mr. Kopfrkingl bowed slightly and left. 'The director,' he said to himself on the staircase, on his way to the cloakroom, 'is uneasy, as if he sensed that something's happening around him. That he's being weighed up and discussed. That he's not going to be here much longer now. He's not a bad fellow,' he said to himself, 'but what's the good of it? We can't put up with evil-doers in this sort of place. Why, nobody would have evil-doers in this sort of place, that's obvious, only human. What he said about cremating the Germans in the ovens, that's . . .' Mr. Kopfrkingl shook his head violently, covered his eyes with his hand and quickened his pace in order to reach the cloakroom as soon as possible. He arrived in the cloakroom and changed his clothes. In front of the furnaces, he smiled at Zajíc and Beran who were watching the thermometers coldly and in silence. From the funeral hall, "My Czech Lands, my beautiful Czech Lands . . ." could be heard through the loudspeaker. He asked them where Mr. Dvořák was, and Zajíc jerked his head towards the preparation room at the end of the corridor.

'You're adjusting the dress,' he smiled at Mr. Dvořák, who was standing over an open coffin in the preparation room and putting flowers on the dead woman. Then he went closer, looked in and said: 'She has a beautiful dress, the sweet one, a black silk dress with a collar, of course. People usually have their best dresses on in the coffin. For example, they put on a dress they've only worn a couple of times during their lifetime, Mr. Dvořák. Everybody wants to look beautiful in the coffin, Mr. Dvořák.'

Then he said:

'This is Miss Vomáčka. She used to sell wine and spirits in a buffet, poor young lady . . . She'll go to the viewing room in a moment. Mr. Pelikán will take her. This coffin,' Mr. Kopfrkingl pointed to the coffin marked with number seven which had been nailed down, 'is nailed down, it will not be put on view. It'll go straight to the funeral hall. A contagious infection. Mr. Kalous . . . You hardly ever smoke now, do you, Mr. Dvořák?' Mr. Kopfrkingl gave a smile and glanced at the iron rod on the floor of the preparation room in front of the niche which was covered by a curtain. 'Well, you've settled down well now. Mr. Pelikán's coming,' he pointed to the door, and when Mr. Pelikán came in with a trolley, Mr. Kopfrkingl glanced once more at the young lady in the coffin, adorned with flowers, nodded at Mr. Pelikán and said: 'You can carry on. Miss Vomáčka is ready . . .'

As Mr. Kopfrkingl was leaving the building, Mr. Fenek crept out of the porter's lodge.

'Mr. Kopfrkingl,' he raised his soft, tear-stained eyes, and both his voice and hand with the long nail on his little finger were shaking, 'isn't the morphia . . .'

'Mr. Fenek,' said Mr. Kopfrkingl rather harshly and stopped. 'If you don't stop pestering me I am going to inform the police. You know that morphine addiction is an offence. It's a perversion which is not compatible with a man's honour. I don't want to hear another word, or else I'll take you to the lunatic asylum.' Then he glanced at Mr. Fenek, who almost staggered, and said a little more kindly:

'I'm not going to give you anything, Mr. Fenek, I'm protecting your health. If you don't have any sense then I must have it for you. I won't have you on my conscience. I'm an honourable and healthy man. I don't even drink or smoke, I'm abstemious, and, as you can see, I'm also alive. Don't bother me any more.'

Mr. Fenek crept back into the porter's lodge, completely crushed. 'Just look at that,' thought Mr. Kopfrkingl and stepped out of the building into the courtyard. 'I've shown him a bit of strength again and it frightened him. Just look at that. How mankind benefits from strength, from a show of character. The weak and inferior are a burden, they can't contribute to the battle for tomorrow.' In the porter's lodge in the courtyard he caught a glimpse of Mr. Vrána, who sat there because he had something wrong with his liver. It seemed to him that as Mr. Vrána spotted him he turned away . . .

When he came home, to the dining-room, his heavenly one was standing by the window, under the picture of the wedding procession and the wall chart, the most sublime timetable. He merely smiled at her black hair, feeling regret at the same time. Then he caught Mili hiding something quickly by the little mirror which was hanging in the dining-room. He saw that it was a photograph, and said to himself, ah, that's life. Not only Zina and that Míla of hers, it's Mili now as well. Well, of course, the children are maturing, growing up . . . He approached the radio and turned it on.

'That poor Mr. Fenek of ours,' he said, 'asked me for morphia again. He's a weak, soft man who's finished . . . it's a perversity. I wonder what's happening to Mr. Prachař and his drinking, and what about his unfortunate son, Vojta? I haven't seen his wife for maybe a year now . . .' Then Almaviva's sweet cavatina from "The Barber", which he sang to Rosina beneath her balcony, could be heard on the radio . . . and Mr. Kopfrkingl turned round, went to Mili standing by the little mirror, and reached out his hand. 'Well, show me your sweetheart,' he extended his hand, 'your first love, so that we can get to know her too . . .' After hesitating a little, Mili gave him the photo. But it was not a girl. It was the butcher's apprentice.

'That's the butcher's apprentice,' Mili faltered and glanced at the cat. 'Well, you know, that boxer.'

After a moment's silence, Mr. Kopfrkingl gave a smile and said: 'How did you get hold of it? You know each other?'

'Why, you sent me to get the programme yourself so that I'd know *who* was going to box . . .' said Mili, and then he revealed that he had twice been to the Youth Club, where they had their training.

'Why,' said Mili, 'it said come and see us . . . Well, that leaflet,' he said, 'that application form which Mr. Reinke gave me . . .'

'But that's wonderful, Mili, to be friends with a boxer,' said Mr. Kopfrkingl after a while, and thought, he's friends with a boxer, perhaps he won't be so soft, so effeminate after all, as Willi says; perhaps he'll get over it. Then he said aloud: 'You must be hard, courageous, one hundred-percent, Mili. After all, you've got German blood. From me . . .' he added knitting his brows. 'After the holidays you'll go to the German grammar school. Well, yes,' he smiled at Lakmé, who was taken aback and looked dejected, and turning back to Mili, who was gazing at the cat. He said:

'It's certainly a good thing to go out with a boxer. Boxing is a combative sport, ein Wettkampf. The Führer considers it one of the best. If only you didn't stray about so much, Mili. You'd better not even go to the bridge. Is that boxer of yours training hard?' he gave a smile, returning the photo to the boy, and when Mili nodded, he said: 'What is he telling you, what do you two talk about . . .'

And then to his horror, he learned what the boxer was telling him, what the two were talking about. Why he was training so hard. Why he was learning so hard how to box. Why his punches had to be driven home. Because the Germans had poured into our country. Because they were bullies. Because they had taken our freedom . . . As he spoke, Mili's face took on a sheepish look and he gazed at the cat. Mr. Kopfrkingl kept control of himself and shook his head sadly. There's still time to enlighten him, he thought, gazing at Mili. I'm going to explain it to him soon, make him see sense, convince him. And he went to the radio, where Almaviva was just finishing his sweet song to Rosina, and lightly pushed the cat aside who had got between his legs.

Before the Whitsun holidays, the Gestapo arrested Josef Zajíc and Beran in the crematorium. Then came the turn of the director, Srnec. 'It seems rather hard,' said Mr. Kopfrkingl, the NSDAP member with the sterling German soul, to himself, 'what the Gestapo has done. But there was probably nothing else to be done about it, nothing at all. After all, the happiness of millions of people is at stake. We'd be committing an offence against the people,' said Mr. Kopfrkingl to himself, 'an offence against mankind if we didn't know how to get rid of evil-doers, if we sat on our hands and just looked on at their destructive work.' So, the Gestapo arrested Zajíc, Beran and the director, Srnec, in the crematorium . . .

Mili and Zina went to Slatiňany for the Whitsun holidays to stay with their good aunt, who, had she been a Catholic, would have been canonized when she died, though she's already a saint: they went to her with a bunch of lilies. It was during those days that a decision on an important matter in Mr. Kopfrkingl's life was to be made: on his promotion.

'My heavenly one,' said Mr. Kopfrkingl to Lakmé in the dining-room, 'the children have gone to Slatiňany for the Whitsun holidays to stay with our aunt, with that good soul of ours, who's already a saint . . . and we're alone. They've arrested Mr. Zajíc, Beran and Srnec, the director, at my workplace . . . God knows why, apparently because of their feelings of hostility towards the Reich, the German people, mankind . . . What?' he smiled at Lakmé, who was horrified, 'why are you frightened? Because they've arrested Zajíc, Beran and the director? Don't worry, nothing's going to happen to them, why should anything happen to them? They'll just transfer them to another place of work . . .' Then he said: 'I'm supposed to become the new director instead of Mr. Srnec. I'm supposed to become director because I'm an expert . . . Since we're on our own now, my dear, how about putting our best clothes on and having a nice little dinner-party? Without wine, of course, I'm abstemious . . . and then we'll have a bath in our beautiful bathroom as is proper after a Roman banquet. Could it be our heavenly wedding anniversary today?' he smiled tenderly. 'Or, at least, the blessed anniversary of the day we met in the zoo by the leopard . . .? No, it isn't. Alright, but let's pretend it is . . . come,' Mr. Kopfrkingl took Lakmé by her arm and led her to the kitchen to get the food ready.

Towards evening, when the food was ready, Mr. Kopfrkingl asked Lakmé to put on her best dark silk dress with the white lace collar. After she had put it on he took her into the dining-room and seated her at the table. He brought sandwiches, almonds, coffee and tea, turned on the radio, and then sat down at the table too.

'Do you hear, my heavenly one?' he smiled tenderly. 'What they're playing now is the chorus and bass from Donizetti's "Lucia di Lammermoor". It's interesting. It's such perfect funeral music, and yet it's not played in our place very often. Anyone having it played in our hall would indeed have an uncommon funeral. They played the "Unfinished" for Mrs. Strunný once, Dvořák's Largo for Miss Čárský, and Friedrich von Flotow's "Last Rose of Summer" for Miss Vomáčka recently. The flaw is that it's not the deceased who choose the music, as a rule, but the mourners! And they don't choose according to the taste of the dead but according to their own. They choose things they like themselves, not what their departed ones would like to have had.' Then he said:

'This is Lucia's big aria from the third act. It's sung by an excellent Italian singer.'

And as they ate to the accompaniment of Lucia's big aria on the radio, Mr. Kopfrkingl said:

'Our life is before us, my *purest one*. The whole world is open for us, my ethereal one. The sky is open for us.' He pointed and glanced at the ceiling as though drawing attention to the stars, a magnificent picture, or an apparition. 'The sky over which not a single little cloud has passed during the whole nineteen years of our being together, the sky I sometimes see over my Temple of Death when nobody is being cremated. But I've noticed that our ventilator in the bathroom is broken. I'll have to have it repaired tomorrow. For the time being I've put a string with a noose in there, so that we'll be able to switch the ventilator on from the chair. That curtain over there in the corner . . .' he pointed to the window, 'which Willi told us about on Christmas Eve, has not been any trouble since. Do you hear that beautiful song?' He pointed to the radio from which the sounds of

Lucia's big aria wafted over to them. 'How very true it is that those who die without ever learning the beauty of music are poor. Where's Rosana, I wonder . . .?'

After dinner, Mr. Kopfrkingl kissed his heavenly one and said:

'Come, my *indescribable one*, before we undress, let's get the bath ready.'

He took the chair and they adjourned, the cat watching them.

'It's hot in here,' said Mr. Kopfrkingl in the bathroom and placed the chair under the ventilator. 'I probably overdid the heating. Switch on the ventilator, my dear.'

When Lakmé got onto the chair, Mr. Kopfrkingl stroked her ankle, cast the noose round her neck and said to her with a tender smile:

'What if I hanged you, my dear?'

She smiled down at him, perhaps not understanding him very well. He returned her smile, kicked the chair away and that was that.

He put on his coat in the hall and went to the German Criminal Investigation Department. He made a statement:

'She apparently did it out of despair. She had Jewish blood and could not bear living by my side. Perhaps she sensed that I was going to divorce her, that it was not compatible with my German honour.' And inwardly, he said to himself: I was sorry for you, my dear, I really was. You were dejected, withdrawn. Of course. No wonder. But as a German I had to make the sacrifice. I've saved you, my dear, from the suffering which would otherwise have been in store for you. My heavenly one, how you would have suffered in the just and happy new world, on account of your blood . . .

Lakmé was cremated in Chrudim near Slatiňany . . . and Mr. Karl Kopfrkingl was – after the Whitsun holidays – appointed director of the Prague crematorium. He *pensioned off* Mr. Vrána of the *porter's lodge* in the courtyard, who sat there because he had something wrong with his liver. He's old now, he thought, he's been here ever since I came, almost twenty years ago. Let him have a rest. He gave notice to Mrs. Podzimek, the cleaning woman, to quit. After all, she was almost frightened here, he said to himself, *I'll rid her of her fear then, of that curse.* . . But he kept Mr. Dvořák. 'You know, Mr. Dvořák, what I like about you is that you don't smoke and drink . . .' he told him, 'that you're abstemious . . .' And he also kept Mr. Pelikán and Mr. Fenek too for the time being. I ought to save him, he sometimes thought to himself in his office, he's hardly able to stand. When he passed the porter's lodge, Mr. Fenek cried, cringing like a dog.

XIV

Yes, what their mother had done was a shock, for the children, but one has to come to terms with all sorts of things in life.

'Life today, my dearest ones,' Mr. Kopfrkingl told his children as he stood under the lamp in the dining-room with the newspaper in his hands, 'life today is one big battle. We live in great, revolutionary times and have to stand up straight in the face of every sacrifice and hardship. Our heavenly one is now among the blessed, like her mother. Gracious Nature freed her from the fetters of this world. She has peacefully returned to where she came from, to dust. The ether has opened for her, and possibly by now she has already entered a new body. Cremation accelerates . . . She was a nice, good woman,' he said with the newspaper in his hands, 'faithful, quiet, modest. The light everlasting is shining for her now, now she is enjoying heavenly peace.' Then with a glance at the newspaper he said:

'Nothing is certain in human life. The future is uncertain, and that's why people are often afraid of it. The only certain thing in life is death. But now it's quite certain that a new, happy order will be established in Europe. The Führer's new happy Europe and death are the only two certainties which we, the people, have today . . . There's a beautiful poem here in the papers . . .' he turned over the pages of the newspaper. 'It seems as if it was written precisely in honour of our departed one. I'll just read the first verse out to you,' he said and read:

'When, at dusk, daylight is wedded to darkness . . .'

Then he glanced at the picture of the wedding procession by the wall chart, the timetable of death, and said, filled with concern:

'Flames cannot hurt any more . . .'

Then he put the newspaper aside, took the book about Tibet out of the bookcase and said:

'I must take even more care of you than before, my gentle ones, now that we've lost our mother. Zina dear . . .' he smiled at his daughter and then glanced at the book about Tibet he was holding in his hand, 'you're beautiful like your mother. You're going out with Míla, but it'll be necessary for you to go to the German school after the holidays. Mili too,' he gave the boy a long, searching look, and then glanced again at the book about Tibet, frowning a little. That boy, with his gentle effeminate soul, worried him more and more. He's never been like me, he thought, with a glance at the book, he's never been like me, and now he's straying even more than before. Let's hope he doesn't wander off somewhere one night so that I have to get the police to search for him as they did that time in Suchdol. Instead of toughening him up and strengthening him, that apprentice of his, the boxer, is misleading him, leading him astray . . . Suppose he ends up like that unfortunate Vojta Prachař in our apartment house. And one day . . .

One day he talked about him to Willi at the Casino, in the presence of the fairhaired beauty, Marie, who looked like an angel or a first-class actress and whom he called *Marlén*.

'Mili's worrying me more and more,' he sighed with a glance at the carpets, pictures and glowing chandeliers. 'He seems to be getting softer and more effeminate all the time. He's never been like me and he is straying more than ever. I'm worried that he'll spend a night in some place like Such-dol again. He didn't learn much from that boxing-match,' he glanced at the glasses filled with cognac on the table, 'we saw the other day, unfortunately. He himself wouldn't box for all the world, and yet it could be useful to him one day, as you said. He apparently learned only one thing from that boxing-match – he made the acquaintance of the butcher's apprentice. But that apprentice of his, the boxer, it seems, is misleading him, leading him astray instead of toughening him up and strengthening the German blood he's inherited from me. It makes me sad. Suppose he ends up,' he glanced at the glasses filled with cognac on the table, 'like that un-fortunate Vojta Prachař from our apartments . . .'

'His mother was half-Jewish,' said Willi and glanced at the fairhaired Marlén, who was leaning on Mr. Kopfrkingl's shoulder. 'And obviously it shows. Milivoj is an individual of mixed blood of the second class. According to the Reich Citizenship Law of 14 November 1935, paragraph 2, he is an individual of mixed Jewish blood of the second class, the so-called quarter-Jew . . . Vierteljude derjenige, der von einem volljüdischen Grosselternteil abstammt. It's the law,' he said gazing at Marlén who was leaning on Mr. Kopfrkingl. 'Laws are here to serve people, as you say, and we must hold them in reverence. I'm afraid, Karl, he won't be admitted to our grammar school. I'm afraid he won't even be admitted to the Hitler Youth. You are sure you won't have a cognac?' he pointed to the glasses on the table, but Mr. Kopfrkingl shook his head, pushing one of them away slightly.

'We're approaching Warsaw,' Marlén gave a laugh.

One Saturday afternoon in the week when the swastika flew over Warsaw and the Reich armed forces were advancing on the East, Mr. Karl Kopfrkingl put on his new high black boots and a green Tyrolean hat with a braid and a feather, which he had only just bought from a German hatter in Můstek. He put a nice little pair of pincers into his pocket and took Mili to see round the crematorium: it was possible to do so, as there was no cremation on a Saturday afternoon. It was beautiful outside. They ran into Jan Bettelheim and Vojta Prachař in front of the house. They were standing there, leaning against the wall and looking at the parked cars. They nooded to Mili, asking him where he was going. Mr. Kopfrkingl halted, smiled affably and said that they were going for a stroll. Mili was gazing at the boys, and they at him as though devising some kind of plan in their minds, and Mr. Kopfrkingl said:

'You must come and see us again some time, boys. You haven't been to see us for such a long time. Only you mustn't go too far when you're outside. Unfortunately, it's not a good time for wandering about nowadays.' Then he smiled again, at the parked cars, and said: 'So, these are the coloured cars according to your theory, aren't they, Mili? The green ones are military and prison vans, and the white ones are ambulances. For angels.' And with a nod to the boys they went on . . . After a few steps Mr. Kopfrkingl said:

'It's possible that we'll also have a nice coloured car soon, Mili. You'll ride in it as Jan Bettelheim used to do. We could go for a drive on Sundays. Somewhere further than Suchdol, of course, to a castle or a mansion-house, for example. You'd like that, I think. Dr. Bettelheim doesn't have a car any longer, unfortunately.' Then they arrived at a pink confectionery shop and Mili halted.

'Well, wait a minute, you sweet-toothed little brute,' Mr. Kopfrkingl gave a smile and delved into the pocket where he had the little pair of pincers. 'Here you are. Buy yourself a choc-ice.' Then he reached into his pocket once more and said: 'Here you are, buy yourself a *chocolate ring* too.'

Mili bought himself a choc-ice and a chocolate ring, and they went on. Near the Vinohrady cemetery some kind of advertisement was posted. A little old fat man was standing under it reading it. As they came nearer, Mr. Kopfrkingl noticed that the little man had a stiff white collar with a red bow tie. As he noticed it, he raised his head a little.

'Pity,' he said to Mili and his voice shook slightly. 'A pity that your heavenly mother's not with us.' Then he noticed the advertisement and felt that some of the letters wanted to jump out of it:

<blockquote>
Drapes and curtains repaired by
JOSEFA BROUČEK, PRAGUE – HLOUBĚTÍN
7 Kateřinská Street
</blockquote>

'We'll go through the cemetery,' he said to Mili. 'It's much nicer to go the back way than through the courtyard. I used to take a stroll here at lunchtime before I became director. A pity that your heavenly mother has been called to meet her Maker.'

As they were going through the cemetery gate, they heard a noise and some cracking sounds beyond the first tombstones, as though somebody was jumping about and hissing. And then a woman with a string of beads and a feather in her hat rushed out at them, pointing behind her and squeaking. A small fat man with a bowler hat and a stick raced after her shouting: 'Where are you dashing off to, you . . . there are *no towers* here, this is a cemetery. You were in a cemetery . . .' and he stopped, shaking his head furiously at Mr. Kopfrkingl, at his high black boots and the green Tyrolean hat with the braid and feather, and said: 'She's a fool, she does it to me all the time. She thought I was taking her out to some kind of massacre . . .'

'She'll get over it, I'm sure,' said Mr. Kopfrkingl kindly, and the fat man took off his hat and began to wipe his forehead.

'Come,' said Mr. Kopfrkingl to Mili kindly. The boy was gaping. 'Probably some kind of fit, she'll get over it. The angel in our midst, the doctor, will help her. Mili,' he said, 'don't ever dream of putting a banger into your mouth. It could land you in big trouble. Did you like the chocolate ring?'

Then they went through the cemetery, passing the graves with wreaths laid on them, and found themselves in front of the crematorium. A little cur with a long nail on his little finger was trembling in the porter's lodge. He saw the director in his high boots and the Tyrolean hat with the feather and bowed, his eyes swollen and tear-stained. 'Will I be able to save him, I wonder?' thought Mr. Kopfrkingl. 'I'll have to dismiss him or help him to get into the lunatic asylum.' He waved his hand at him and went on. He led Mili into the corridor, to the cloakroom, to the extinguished furnaces. The place smelled of lysol and the boy was shaking like a leaf.

'So, these are the ovens,' he said, shaking and gazing uncertainly.

'That's them,' Mr. Kopfrkingl gave a smile. 'Don't tell me you're frightened. Why, they're empty. Why, nobody is being cremated. You're always frightened,' he gave a smile, 'whenever we go somewhere, Mili. I don't know who you've inherited it from. You were frightened in the waxworks some time ago, you were frightened when we went to see the boxing-match, and you were frightened in the lookout tower . . . did something happen to you then . . .?' Then he said:

'Here are the buttons for the iron curtain in the funeral hall. Here are the thermometers, and here's the loudspeaker so that the employees can listen to the music . . . So, these

(161)

are our fine mechanisms, and automatic processes . . . On that scaffold over there, in the ovens, are little windows of smoked glass, but you don't really have to see them . . . Here's the chart which you know. Wait, I'll have a look . . .' Then they passed the storage place for the tin cylinders used for ashes, with their calibre of 16 cm and height of 23 cm. It smelled of lysol, and the boy was shaking like a leaf . . . 'That's the storage place for the cylinders used for ashes,' said Mr. Kopfrkingl. 'They're standardized . . .' And then they entered the preparation room with the coffins.

'Here you can see Mr. Daněk,' Mr. Kopfrkingl gave a smile. 'Here Dr. Veverka, his coffin is rather narrow. Poor thing, when they put the lid on, it'll rest on his forehead. Here's Mr. Piskoř with his *angel's* wing . . . he died of rickets . . . but that doesn't matter. I'll show you this coffin,' Mr. Kopfrkingl gave a smile and went to a coffin which was nailed down, bearing the number 5 and the name of E. Wagner. 'It's nailed down because it won't be opened again. It won't be put on view but will go straight from here into the funeral hall on Monday.' Mr. Kopfrkingl took the little pair of pincers out of his pocket and opened the lid.

A sharp, pale emaciated face in a full-dress, grey-green uniform was revealed in the coffin. It had the Iron Cross on its chest, a peaked cap and white gloves. There was a laurel sprig in its buttonhole. Another sprig, possibly myrtle, was resting on its hands which were folded on his stomach.

'This is Mr. Ernst *Wagner*,' said Mr. Kopfrkingl to the boy, who was shaking like a leaf and desperately squeezing his own hands. 'SS Sturmbannführer . . . he was fond of his people and of *music*. He'll be laid to rest to the sounds of Wagner's "Parsifal". So, that boxer of yours is going to beat up the Germans?' Mr. Kopfrkingl smiled sadly at his terrified son. 'The bullies, the intruders. You've probably told him that you like sweets because *he takes you to confectionery shops*, doesn't he . . .? Look here, this Mr. Wagner is a thoroughbred German. He's no soft, effeminate soul . . . he's of pure origin. Ohne Rücksicht auf den Dienstgrad muss jeder SS-Angehörige den Abstammungsnachweis erbringen, wenn er sich verloben oder verheiraten will. This is what the Reich Law says. You know what it means in Czech . . .? Well, that regardless of rank, every SS member must produce a certificate of ancestry when *he wants to get engaged or married* . . . Laws are here to help people . . .' Mr. Kopfrkingl gave a smile and then he said: 'His coffin is as it should be, high and wide enough. What if you were to lie next to him, Mili? Lie next to him and be melted down, you and he together, to the sounds of "Parsifal" on Monday?' And with a less than cheerful smile, he took the *iron rod* which lay in the corner by the niche with the curtain, *forced the boy down on his knees, and standing astride over him* in his high black boots and Tyrolean hat with the braid and the *feather*, he battered him with the rod. Then he lifted him from the floor and shoved him next to the SS man. The coffin was, as it should be, high and wide. It held them both like two very different brothers. He nailed down the coffin with the little pair of pincers, checked both the rod and tiles to see that they were clean, adjusted his hat . . . and went out. 'Death unites,' he said to himself, with his hand resting on the little pair of pincers in his pocket. 'There's no difference in human ashes. It doesn't matter whether they are the ashes of a German Bannführer or of a quarter-Jewish boy. Poor boy,' he said to himself. 'How he would have suffered in his life otherwise. The things I have spared that good boy. He wouldn't have been admitted to German schools, nor into the Hitler Youth now, let alone into the happy, new order when it comes. The only pity is I didn't manage to take a picture of him . . .'

'. . . Mili, don't run away, wait for me,' he called out in front of Mr. Fenek's porter's lodge so as to be heard inside, in the little room. Mr. Fenek was there, at that very moment, cowering, with his lips on his hand as though kissing it, his eyes dim. 'Mr. Fenek,' he said to him, 'you're licking your hand! You must have some medical treatment, Mr. Fenek. You can't go on like this. You're not going to ruin your life, are you? What you're doing is Abartigkeit, monstrous. How about a psychiatrist?' and Mr. Fenek raised his head, burst into tears and wrung his hands. Mr. Kopfrkingl then stepped out of the building and crossed the courtyard to the porter's lodge, where he was greeted reverently by Mr. Vrána's successor. In front of the courtyard gate he gave a twenty-heller coin to the old beggarwoman, who stood there not only on Fridays, but on Saturdays too, all the year round. She looked like a white figure of Fate. He headed for the tram. A young pink-faced girl in a black dress was standing there with a young man, with a camera strapped over his shoulder.

Four days later, Mr. Kopfrkingl went to the German Criminal Investigation Department to report that his sixteen-year-old son was missing.

'It's been four days now and he hasn't come back,' he said. 'He's been doing it to us ever since he was small. We even had the police search for him once. They had to go all the way to Suchdol to find him. He wanted to spend the night in a haystack there. He had all kinds of romantic ideas. I'm worried that he might have set out to join our army in Poland. He's also been going about with a boxer lately.' Mili had by then been mingled with the ashes of the thoroughbred SS man for four days. The act had been carried out by the director himself. Assisted by the understanding and accommodating smiles of the two who had been taken on to replace Zajíc and Beran, he refreshed his expert knowledge in front of the furnace, and, at the same time, showed his respect for their work: work such as he had started himself as a son of rather ordinary parents. This was accompanied by the funeral march from Beethoven's "Eroica". Before that by Wagner's "Parsifal".

Following the victorious military campaign in Poland, Mr. Kopfrkingl was summoned to see Boehrmann, the head of the Prague Sicherheitsdienst and secretary of the Reich Protector — to Boehrmann in that light-coloured, broad building with the pillars and all the cars in front, and the Reich flag flying over it. Summoned to his office which smelled sweetly of sandalwood and contained several magnificent pictures as well as beautiful curtains, a thick carpet and a big portrait of the Führer. And here, in the office of the head of the Prague Sicherheitsdienst and the secretary of the Reich Protector, he was told in confidence about an experiment which was important to them. It was the autumn of 1939.

'Here's to the purification and honour of the German people. Here's to the victorious struggle for a new happy Europe. Here's to just world order, the Führer's new order,' they told him and lifted their glasses from the shiny table, revealing some kind of book lying behind them. Willi Reinke was also there, and asked him: 'Can I give you something? Cognac? Czech plum brandy . . .?' Then they told him:

'You've got experience. You're fond of mechanisms and automation. You're a proud champion of Teutonism. We need to try out gas furnaces, you know, so eine treffliche Gaseinrichtung für die Zukunft. But *utter discretion* is necessary, *it's secret*. You are being offered a great honour. You could be the expert in charge.'

'Sort of gas furnaces for the future,' repeated Willi and lightly touched the book resting on the shiny table top, 'For the future which is always uncertain except for death and our victory. *Not even horses* are going to suffer,' he gave a smile. 'You are being offered an honour. This is,' he said, 'what I promised you when you were a beggar in Maislova Street. You'll get a Mercedes saloon. You'll be able to,' he gave a smile, 'take your family for a drive . . .' Then he gave a smile, raised the glass and said: 'You have been *chosen*. Are you sure you still don't drink . . .?'

And with a smile, Mr. Kopfrkingl inhaled the sweet smell of the sandalwood, which permeated the office of the head of the Prague Sicherheitsdienst and secretary of the Reich Protector, glanced at the book behind the glasses and placed his hands on his lap. 'Thank you, gentlemen,' he said and shook his head. 'Indeed, I still don't drink. I don't drink alcohol, I'm abstemious.' And he accepted the honour offered to him.

And then he paid visits to the Casino, through its miraculous entrance with the three steps, covered with white marble. He had fairhaired mistresses, particularly Marlén, whose original name was Marie, and who looked like an angel or a first-class actress. He had about ten or twenty of them and visited them elsewhere too, and not only in the Casino, though never in the Malvaz pub, for he had stopped going there long ago. Some of them came to see him in his apartment in return. He had so many of them that he almost mixed them up. On the other hand, he did not drink or smoke, he was abstemious. He was sorry for those who did not have such beauties. He was sorry for Mrs. Prachař, whose husband had become addicted to alcohol, and for their unfortunate son, Vojta, who could inherit it from him. He was also sorry for the others, Dr. Bettelheim and his family for example, who no longer had either his car or his surgery. In the dining-room, he often gazed towards the window, at the picture of the wedding procession, which he had bought for Zina in Mr. Holý's picture-framing shop on Nekázanka Street some time ago, and at the wall chart on the cord beside it, that most sublime timetable on earth, the timetable of death. He often gazed at the spot over the dining-room door where the Führer, a perfect print of a perfect gentleman, had been hanging for a long time instead of the Nicaraguan president, and he often said to himself, 'I'll get a letter soon appointing me head of the experiment, of the gas furnaces, and the Mercedes car . . .' He also gazed at the family photograph over the cabinet, in which he was sitting next to Lakmé, between the children with the cat on his lap . . . He would also go to the adjoining living-room and gaze at the spot over the piano, where the glass box with the flies was hanging, the glass box with the drosophila funebris and fruit or vinegar flies, which had been used in the study of genetics while they were alive. And one ·day – it was towards evening – he recalled the aunt from Slatiňany, that good soul, who, had she been a Catholic, would certainly have been canonized when she died, and who was already a saint, and said to himself: 'I must go to that beautiful dear bathroom of ours I'm so fond of . . .' and he went in. *He lit a candle by the butterfly under the ventilator* . . . Then he returned to the dining-room and switched on the standard lamp because it was already getting dark. He took the law on cremation out of the bookcase and turned over the pages for a while. And then he took out, perhaps for the hundredth time, the book about Tibet . . . that sweet, fascinating book about Tibet, about Tibetan monasteries, the Dalai Lama and his reincarnation, and said to himself, 'Why, I know it almost by heart now . . .' and he went with it to sit down under the lighted lamp. When he opened it, he said to himself, 'But I'm still looking after my sweet enchantingly beautiful one; God be thanked that they let her into the German school. Nevertheless, she does have some of her late mother's features, that eighteen-year-old blackhaired beauty of mine . . .' And then somebody rang the bell.

Under the lamp, Mr. Kopfrkingl rose to his feet, put the Tibetan book on the dining-table and went to open the door.

'Can I speak to Director Kopfrkingl?' said the visitor at the door in German. 'I've been sent here, it's confidential . . .' Mr. Kopfrkingl gave a bow and stepped aside for the visitor to enter. He then led him to the dining-room. The caller's face was rather yellow, though this could have been the effect of the light from the standard lamp. However, he wore rather strange clothes, something like a black frock.

'Would you care to sit down?' Mr. Kopfrkingl motioned to the table without revealing any sign of surprise. 'Excuse me . . .' and he picked up the book which was lying there, 'I've just been reading a book . . . Can I give you something? *Cognac, Czech plum brandy* . . .' he said politely.

'No, thank you,' smiled the visitor and put his hands into his lap. 'I don't drink alcohol. I don't smoke either. I'm abstemious . . .' and then he smiled again and said:

'If I may, I'd like some tea and a little piece of butter . . .' And after Mr Kopfrkingl had rushed into the kitchen, made the tea with a little piece of butter in it and brought it back to the dining-room, the visitor glanced at him and said:

'*Kushog* I'm a *tulku* from the Mindoling monastery. Our Dalai Lama is dead. Tibet, our blessed country, has been searching for his incarnation for years . . . seventeen, nineteen years. The incarnation of the great man whom Buddha has *chosen*, in whom he has been *reincarnated*, and . . . found him at last, after so many years of quest and search, after almost twenty years. I've been sent on this long journey to find you and tell you that it's *you*. The throne in Lhasa is waiting for you, *rimpoche*.'

Then he said:

'But *utter discretion* is necessary, *it's secret* . . . I shall come here again several times to initiate you. Then we'll leave for the Himalayas, for our paradise, our blessed country . . .'

'Father, you've had visitors,' said Zina when she returned home. 'There are two cups on the table and there's some butter *at the bottom* of one of them.'

'I've had a distinguished visitor here, my dear,' said Mr. Kopfrkingl watching her. 'But you mustn't talk about it, mustn't let on. It's secret. Utter discretion is necessary.

How do you like the school, my own beautiful one? Your new German school?'

'I've lost my friends,' said Zina dejectedly. 'I didn't know I'd lose them. I thought everything would be as it was before. I don't see Lenka and Lála any more . . .'

'They were good, nice class-mates,' Mr. Kopfrkingl gave a nod. 'But what can you do? You lose all kinds of things. How many tragedies I've seen in my life already,' he said. 'Mrs. Strunný, Miss Čárský, Miss Vomáčka, Mrs. Liška, Mrs. Podzimek. Mr. Holý who lost his wife; Mr. Rubinstein who got himself a divorce; Mr. Strauss whose wife died of consumption of the throat and his son of scarlet fever . . . in fact, you lose all the time, that's our lot. What about Mr. Míla Janáček . . .'

'He hasn't said anything so far, but I think we'll break up,' said Zina.

'You'll break up,' Mr. Kopfrkingl gave a nod and glanced at the family picture over the cabinet. 'There you are. He was a good, nice boy, from a good, decent family. His father was a mechanical engineer; he himself was fond of physics and machines; he was, like me, fond of music and various mechanisms and automatic processes. His future was before him. It's a pity. At least you have these photographs to remind you of him forever.' He pointed to the picture above the cabinet. Glancing at it, Zina said:

'Still no news about Mili?'

'No, my little girl, no. My God, where is he . . .?' Mr. Kopfrkingl frowned and sat down.

She stroked his hair sadly, and he took her hand and said: 'We live in great, revolutionary times, and we still have a lot of worries. We all lose. Dr. Bettelheim . . .' he pointed to the ceiling where the doctor used to have his surgery, 'is no longer allowed to carry on his profession. Nach der . . . durch die . . . vom 25. 7. 1938 sind Juden von der Ausübung der ärztlichen Tätigkeit im Deutschen Reich grundsätzlich ausgeschlossen. All Jews in the German Reich are, irrevocably, excluded from carrying out medical practice . . . it's the law, and as you know, we have to respect the law . . . It's true, he still lives above us, up there, in two apartments, with his beautiful wife, Anežka and his nephew, Jan. He has an old, magnificent picture in his former surgery, of some kind of *abduction* of a woman by Count Bethlén, but that's all he's got. His car's no longer in front of the house. But there'll be another one soon, a beautiful Mercedes, and it'll be *ours*. And on that wall over there . . .' he pointed to one of the dining-room walls, 'a magnificent old picture will be hanging. But that's a trifle, he said quickly. 'After all, it's completely insignificant what is and what's not going to hang there. One mustn't become a slave to one's *own* possessions. We live in great, revolutionary times, my beauty, and it's necessary to think of the whole. Of the nation, of mankind. What is an individual compared with it . . .? Don't let *this*,' he tenderly stroked Zina's hair, apparently thinking of Zina's break-up with Míla, 'bother you, my heavenly one. The Czechs will be liquidated. Yes, my child, that's the way things are now,' he said when Zina started up. 'We must face the truth courageously and openly. There's no point in concealing things, my dear. If we are able to bear the death of our departed one and now the misfortune with Mili, then we should be able to bear this too. It is in the interest of our people and mankind to liquidate the Czechs. In the interest of the happy and just new order which is being built by the Führer. They're not going to perish physically, no, they're not,' Mr. Kopfrkingl shook his head and raised his hands. 'They're not going to perish physically, *we aren't murderers*. But they'll be Germanized. It's in the interest of our people and a happy Europe. This is our very own living space and we'll run the world from here,' he pointed with his hand round the dining-room and glanced at the cat, who had just made her appearance. 'When this happens there'll be paradise. For ever.'

A few days later, Mr. Kopfrkingl said to Zina, who was about to go to her piano lesson:

'My lovely! A letter came for me. I've been appointed head of an enormous undertaking. I'm leaving the crematorium for a higher post. It concerns a Reich project which will prevent the exploitation of mankind once and for all, its suffering from hunger and poverty. It'll rid people of all kinds of suffering, and perhaps even horses . . . Unfortunately, I can't give you any details. It's secret. Utter discretion is necessary. But what if I showed you the place where I've been working for the last twenty years before I leave the crematorium? What would you say to that? To see where your father began, worked, faithfully performed his duties, grew and matured? Tomorrow is Saturday, there's no cremation in the afternoon, not until Monday . . . How about putting on that pretty black silk dress which I bought for you the other day, and going to have a look . . .? I'll get,' he said, 'a camera somewhere . . .'

After Zina had left, the Tibetan envoy paid him a visit. He made tea with butter.

'Rimpoche,' the monk kneeled down before him on the carpet in the dining-room, 'it's time. The throne is waiting for you. Tibet, our blessed country, is waiting for her high priest. The people are waiting for their ruler. Here is the robe of the last Lama . . .' The monk pointed with his hand into the empty space as if pointing to stars which were in the dining-room and were not visible. 'Here's the golden *tegag* and the dark red *shamthav*. The wall which obstructed your view has collapsed. The sky has opened, there are infinite stars above us . . .' he pointed to the ceiling . . . 'You're going to save the world. Kyab su chiwo, kyabgön rimpoche.' The monk touched the floor with his forehead. *'You're the Buddha!'*

'Get up, my son,' Mr. Kopfrkingl motioned to the monk benignly, almost with tears in his eyes. Then he positioned himself behind the table, raised his hands as if to the sky, towards the ceiling . . . and said:

'The sky has opened, there are infinite stars above us. *Lags so.* Just as I have read for years in the book by Madame David-Neel, in her book about Tibet, which Mr. Rudolf Kádner, the bookbinder, bound for me in beautiful yellow covers in Ovocný trh, in this city of Prague. May all beings be happy. In the name of the happiness which will come to mankind, no sacrifice is too great for me. Mr. Holý from Nekázanka Street also lost his wife. As did Mr. Strauss, from consumption of the throat, and his son from scarlet fever. But I have yet to do one more thing,' he smiled towards his feet. 'I still have to deliver one good soul. Tomorrow, on Saturday afternoon, I have to send one soul back whence it came, in time to save her from the suffering which awaits her in the future, happy world. She's going to take her dark silk dress and lie down in it next to the greatest pianist there has ever been in Prague, Mrs. Hermína *Sýkora.* The celestial birds are going to sing the second movement from Chopin's piano concerto to her, as laid down by her widower. Wait till tomorrow evening, my son.'

The monk gave a smile and at that moment it was as if the world misted over for Mr. Kopfrkingl. But it was a mist in his own soul. When he had collected himself a little, he heard beautiful music. It was the big aria from Donizetti's "Lucia", the piano concerto, the "Unfinished", "Parsifal" and the "Eroica" . . . and then some lively music, clarinet, fiddles and the double-bass as well, and then some tambourines, kettle drums and prayer wheels. And he saw that three men in white were standing in the dining-room, near the cat and the door with the portrait of the Führer and Reich Chancellor; three *angels*, one of whom was called Piskoř. . . and then they lead him out of the fiat with heavenly kindness, down the stairs, while a terrified lady and her son stepped aside to let them pass . . . out of the apartment house. Out of the apartment house, with a car standing in front of it. A white car, the car for angels, adorned with a red cross and a German number plate. A faint autumn breeze stirred his hair as he bent his head to get in.

In mid-May of 1945 – after the war – through the window of a hospital train, in the railway station of a small German town, Mr. Kopfrkingl saw crowds of emaciated people returning home. It seemed to him that he recognized some familiar faces among them: the faces of a Mr. Strauss and a Mr. Rubinstein, and the old face of Dr. Bettelheim and a young man, possibly his Jan, and some woman too, who seemed familiar to him. He was smiling and he would have liked to wave at them, but his hand was in his pocket at that precise moment, and had just felt something in it. It was a piece of a string and a lump of sugar. And so he merely turned round in the compartment and said to the handless and legless:

'Happy mankind. I've delivered it. There certainly won't be any more persecution, injustice or suffering in the world. No more, for certain, not even for horses . . . Gentlemen, the new order is now beginning.'

Yellowish smoke was rising from the chimney of the Prague crematorium. At that very moment a morphine addict was being cremated.

Fuks's *The Cremator*, published in 1967, marks the high point of the 1960s literary re-evaluation of the Czechs' Second World War experience. Following the Soviet-led military intervention of August 1968, this process would not be publicly resumed in Czechoslovakia until after the fall of Communism. Like other countries occupied by Hitler's Germany, in the immediate aftermath of liberation in 1945, the narrative in the Czech press, literature and cinema had presented the Czechs as innocent victims of brutal Germans, while masking the extent of Czech accommodation with the occupier. The dominance of the Communist Party in post-war politics and culture ensured an exaggerated account of domestic working-class resistance, while attributing any collaboration to the middle-class. From the late 1950s, however, again as in other European countries, a new generation of writers, who had experienced the war as children or adolescents, returned to the subject, sceptical of the prevailing simple picture of the period. Famous examples available to English-speaking readers include Josef Škvorecký's *The Cowards* and the somewhat older Bohumil Hrabal's *Closely Observed Trains*.

Fuks, who was born in 1923 and died in 1994, established himself in the 1960s as the leading Czech literary interpreter of the Occupation with four books, culminating in *The Cremator*. (The literal translation of the Czech title is 'The incinerator of corpses'.) His first, *Mr Theodor Mundstock*, published in 1963 and also available in English translation, describes the preparations made by an elderly Prague Jew as he waits to be deported to Auschwitz. The next two – the short story cycle *My black-haired brothers* (1964) and *Variations for a dark string* (1965) – are both more obviously autobiographical, focusing on how an anxious adolescent with a feverish imagination apprehends of the Occupation and the fate of Jewish boys in his class.

At the time, the most celebrated Czech writer about the period was Arnošt Lustig, an Auschwitz survivor, whose fiction fits more squarely in the genre of 'Holocaust literature' in its focus on Jews and the camps, and its Existentialist-influenced search for glimpses of a positive, even heroic humanity amid the barbarity. Fuks, however, turns the focus on life in Prague, the centre of the Occupation. His narratives lack the implied strong, stable underlying interpretation of events and characters found in earlier treatments of the period. Instead, they examine the psychological impact of the Occupation on fragile, fearful minds that are uncertain how to make sense of or respond to what is happening. Fuks communicates this destabilized, chaotic experience of the world through disorientating narration, grotesque imagery, fluctuation between the real and imagined, and recurring motifs that suggest the possibility of an unreachable, hidden pattern or order beyond the absurdity. His portrayal makes the reader question the sanity of the character or the world in which they live. At the same time, however, these techniques, self-consciously exaggerated in *The Cremator*, show Fuks to be a playful writer, unflinchingly ready to expose the 'human comedy' behind the tragedy.

The Cremator differs from both Fuks's earlier work and previous writing about the Occupation by focusing on a character who collaborates. In keeping with prevailing ideological expectations, Kopfrkingl is petty bourgeois. The perception of working-class Czechs as innocent victims is intensified by the use for crematorium employees of common surnames denoting small, relatively harmless animals that often feature in fables: Beran (Lamb), Liška (Fox), Vrána (Crow), Zajíc (Hare). In accordance with the post-war demonization of Bohemian Germans, over two million of whom were expelled from Czechoslovakia between 1945 and 1947, Willi Reinke is a one-dimensional Devil figure, by turns threatening and tempting Kopfrkingl. Previously, however, collaborators in Czech fiction had been shadowy, minor characters. Fuks, by contrast, places his collaborator at the centre of the novel and asks the reader to accompany him closely on his transition from eccentric but well-intentioned family man to murderer of his wife and son. Perhaps most radically, it is not clear at the end of the novel whether Kopfrkingl will face justice for his actions, or whether – as, in fact, sometimes happened with Nazi collaborators – he will find his way to serving the coming Stalinist regime in Czechoslovakia.

Fuks thus, almost uniquely among Czech writers, manages to draw Kopfrkingl's story out of the Occupation and into a more universal context. Czech readers in 1967 could hardly fail to recognize Kopfrkingl's situation as an allegory for their own under Communist dictatorship, even though any identification of communism with Fascism was taboo. As a writer, but also as a devout Roman Catholic and homosexual in times deeply hostile to both, Fuks well understood the internal conflict between resistance and conformity, expression and repression, and indeed in the 1970s he was himself criticized for collaborating with the Moscow-ordained Party leadership by continuing to publish when many others could not or chose not to. Fuks's novels repeatedly explore the nature of strength and weakness; in *The Cremator*, Willi tells Kopfrkingl: 'There is often greater evil in weakness than in strength', yet Fuks frequently portrays the resilience of the apparently weak. He often sets physically strong, daunting, strident, coldly logical masculinity, embodied in *The Cremator* by Willi, but in other novels by distant, austere fathers, against physically weak, introverted boys or child-like men and women, who resist at least for a time by retreating from an unloving society into elaborate inner worlds.

Kopfrkingl constitutes a negative version of this type. At the beginning of the novel, Kopfrkingl is a peculiar but far from bad man, who wants the best for his family and is deeply troubled by the violence and cruelty of the world, which he seeks to make more benign by renaming things. His Jewish doctor, Bettelheim, a counterweight to Willi, suggests that he needs to accept pain and suffering as inevitable and essential to mortal existence, but Kopfrkingl's love for his family and his yearning for a better world – embodied by the perfection of the crematorium timetable – prove his key weaknesses. Indeed, his decision to collaborate seems motivated more by these than by a desire to ensure his own survival or well-being under the Occupation, though he prospers as a result. The killings may be understood either as a prescient attempt to save his wife and son from the suffering they will undergo once their Jewish blood is discovered, or the liberation of their souls from imprisonment in what Willi tells him is a decaying Jewish body. Fuks's perception that the pursuit of perfection only leads to greater misery and brutality, also found in Hrabal's major works from the 1970s, is a lesson learned from personal experience of two forms of totalitarian ideology, but was and remains unfashionable in a twentieth- and twenty-first developed world predicated on modernization and progress.

The Cremator was met with widespread critical debate and acclaim on publication, and has become a classic of twentieth-century Czech literature. It quickly attracted the attention of the Slovak Jewish film-maker, Juraj Herz, a concentration camp survivor, who claims to have been disappointed with the novel after the promise of its title. Fuks wrote the screenplay, but the film lacks the ambiguity of the novel, and the blackly comic tone of the novel are subordinated to elements of psychological thriller and horror. Evil is nascent in Kopfrkingl from the opening scenes; he attracts no empathy, and is not so much changed as inspired by his encounters with Willi. One might attribute the changes to Herz's own experiences, or the changed context; while the novel was written at a time of increasing liberalization, the film was shot before and after the Soviet-led military intervention, which signalled the defeat of reform-Communism. Indeed, Herz was apparently prevented from using shots of the Soviet army in 1968 to represent the liberation in 1945. The film was withdrawn from cinemas soon after its release in March 1969, but is now widely considered one of Czechoslovak cinema's finest. With this re-publication, English-speaking audiences familiar with the film will once again be able to compare it to the original novel.

Despite its critical reputation, *The Cremator* remains an emotionally difficult text not only for Czech readers. This translation was originally published by Marion Boyars in 1984, at a time of unparalleled popularity for Czech writing by contemporaries of Fuks like Škvorecký, Václav Havel, Ivan Klíma and Milan Kundera, but did not make the same impact. Both at home and abroad, *The Cremator* – similarly but more sharply than Hrabal's *I Served the King of England* – challenges the conventional idea of the Czechs not only as victims, but also as plucky survivors and resisters, which underpinned international imaginings of them especially after 1968. The novel will extend readers' understanding of both the historical context and – as an example of writing not from the liberal centre-left, which draws instead on 'techniques of strangeness' reminiscent of Czech Baroque and Decadent aesthetics – the breadth and depth of Czech literature. Above all, however, Fuks's unique artistic vision deserves at last to take its place in world literature about both the Second World War and the fate of the individual human being amid the oppressive ideologies of the twentieth century and beyond.

Rajendra A. Chitnis
University of Bristol

TRANSLATOR'S NOTE
AND ACKNOWLEDGMENTS

Ladislav Fuks employs metaphors, symbolic characters and motifs. I have tried to preserve as much of the original tone, style and language as possible except in the case of Czech surnames which I have left unchanged.

The names of the employees of the crematorium and some of the dead are names of animals and composers, or names with musical meaning. They are listed with the English translation as follows:

Beran	Ram
Daněk	Fallow deer
Fenek	Desert fox
Liška	Fox
Pelikán	Pelican
Piskoř	Weather loach
Sýkora	Great tit
Srnec	Roebuck
Strunný	Stringed
Veverka	Squirrel
Vlk	Wolf
Vrána	Crow
Zajíc	Hare

There are a few sentences in German in the original which I have also left unchanged in the translation.

I would like to thank my friends, Sue Gilbert and Lionel Munby, for reading the English text and for their helpful comments on the translation. My thanks also go to Richard Hockaday for his support.

ABOUT THE TRANSLATOR

Eva Kandler is an IT consultant. She was born in Nottingham, educated in Prague and is a graduate of Girton College, Cambridge. She has translated prose and poetry and scientific papers from Czech and German.

Central European modern history is notable for many political and cultural discontinuities and often violent changes as well as many attempts to preserve and (re)invent traditional cultural identities. This series cultivates contemporary translations of influential literary works into English (and other languages) which have not been available to global readership due to censorship, the effects of Cold War or repetitive political disruptions in Czech publishing and its international ties.

Readers in English both in today's cosmopolitan Prague or anywhere in the physical and electronic world can thus become acquainted with works which capture the Central European historical experience and which express and also have helped to form Czech and Central European nature, humour and imagination.

Believing that any literary canon can be defined only in dialogue with other cultures, the series will bring proven classics used in Western university courses as well as (re)discoveries aiming to provide new perspectives in intermedial areal studies of literature, history and culture.

All titles are accompanied by an afterword, the translations are reviewed and circulated in the scholarly community before publication which has been reflected by nominations for several literary awards.

Modern Czech Classics series edited by Martin Janeček
and Karolinum Press

Published titles
Zdeněk Jirotka: Saturnin (2003, 2005, 2009, 2013; pb 2016)
Vladislav Vančura: Summer of Caprice (2006; pb 2016)
Karel Poláček: We Were a Handful (2007; pb 2016)
Bohumil Hrabal: Pirouettes on a Postage Stamp (2008)
Karel Michal: Everyday Spooks (2008)
Eduard Bass: The Chattertooth Eleven (2009)
Jaroslav Hašek: Behind the Lines. Bugulma and Other Stories (2012; pb 2016)
Bohumil Hrabal: Rambling On (2014; pb 2016)
Ladislav Fuks: Of Mice and Mooshaber (2014)
Josef Jedlička: Midway Upon the Journey of Our Life (2016)
Jaroslav Durych: God's Rainbow (2016)
Ladislav Fuks: The Cremator (2016)

In Translation
Bohuslav Reynek: The Well at Morning
Ludvík Vaculík: Czech Dreambook
Jan Čep: Short Stories
Viktor Dyk: The Pied Piper